DOG-EARED DELINQUENT

PET WHISPERER P I

BOOK 4

MOLLY FITZ

Editor: Megan Harris
Proofreader: Jasmine Jordan & Tabitha Kocsis
Cover Designer: Lou Harper, Cover Affairs

Whiskered Mysteries
https://whiskeredmysteries.com/

ABOUT THIS BOOK

Apparently I've been slacking on the job as a paralegal, even though the firm doesn't know that I'm secretly working as the area's premier Pet Whisperer P.I. to solve our toughest cases behind the scenes. Now they've hired an intern to "help" me manage my workload...

But what the partners don't realize is that they've let a nefarious criminal into our offices. Trust me, Octo-Cat can smell this guy's stink from a mile away. The worst part? I'm pretty sure he can talk to animals too... and he most definitely isn't using his talents to solve crimes and defend the innocent.

I've always wondered how that zap from an old

coffee maker landed me with supernatural abilities. Now it's time to find out once and for all. Otherwise I fear I may wind up losing them–and my trusty talking feline sidekick–for good.

* * *

To anyone who wishes she could talk to her animal best friend... Well, what's stopping you?

AN INVITE

Hi, I'm Molly Fitz, and I must do whatever the feline overlords demand of me. These days they insist I give them a voice by telling their stories—often with a healthy dose of mystery and always with an uproarious amount of humor.

If you ever wished you could converse with cats, here's your opportunity! This is me officially inviting you into my whacky inner world as part of my Cozy Kitty Club.

For those who just can't get enough of my zany cat characters and their hapless humans, this club will provide weekly (sometimes daily) new content to devour.

From early access to exclusive stories, behind-the-scenes trivia to never-before-released bonus content, and even some signed books and swag thrown in for fun, the CKC has a lot to love.

Come check it out at **www.MollyMysteries.com/club**.

Hope to see you there!

Molly

1

Hi, I'm Angie Russo, and my life is way harder than you'd expect for someone who lives in an old East Coast mansion. Well, it's not really my house— more like my cat's. After all, it's his trust fund that pays the bills.

It may seem like I've won the lottery but think again. Times are tricky when you have a talking cat bossing you around day-in and day-out.

Yeah, I said it.

My cat can talk.

As in, we communicate, have conversations, understand each other. I'm not sure how or why our strange connection works, only that it does. And as much as I wished I knew more, sometimes you just have to accept things at face value. It all happened so fast, too. I went to work unable to talk to animals, got zapped by a faulty coffee maker, got knocked unconscious, and when I woke up again—*bada bing, bada boom!*—now I'm talking kitty.

I've decided to think of it as a stroke of fate, because it really does feel like Octo-Cat and I were meant to find each other. In the past six months alone, we've worked together to solve three separate murder investigations. I guess that's why I'm considering my mom's advice and officially looking into starting a business. She's dubbed me Pet Whisperer P.I.—not because I want anyone else to know about my strange abilities, but because we needed some kind of excuse for me to take Octo-Cat around on my sleuthing calls.

After all, I wouldn't be much of a Sherlock without my Watson. Okay, *I'm* probably the Watson in our relationship. If you've ever been owned by a cat, then you should understand.

Regardless, I'll be the first to admit that my whole life changed for the better once Octo-Cat became a part of it. Before then, I was just drifting from one thing to the next. I'd already racked up seven associate degrees, due to my unwillingness to commit to any one major long enough to secure a bachelor's.

I guess you could say nothing ever felt quite like the perfect fit, but I kept trying anyway. I knew that somewhere out there my dream job was waiting... even if I didn't quite know what it was yet.

You see, greatness kind of runs in my family, and for the longest time I'd worried that particular trait had skipped right past me without a second thought.

My nan had followed her dreams to become a Broadway star back in her glory days, and my mom was the most respected news anchor in all of Blueberry Bay. My dad lived his dream, too, by doing the sports report on the same channel that featured Mom.

Now at last, after so much yearning, so much searching, wishing, and praying, I've found the career path that fits me like a glove—and that's private investigating. So what if I'm not getting paid for it yet? I probably could if I threw everything I had at getting my P.I. business up and off the ground.

But I'm scared of letting down the good people of Longfellow, Peters, & Associates. Oh, that's right. My favorite frenemy Bethany is the newest partner, and I am so proud of her. Between her and Charles, I know the firm is in the best possible hands, but quitting to pursue self-employment?

That's downright terrifying.

True, I'm only part-time at the moment, but the twenty hours per week I put in are really well spent. I know I'm making a difference, and yet...

Aargh. I've never had this much trouble quitting a job before. Why can't I just hand in my two weeks' notice and say, "See ya around?"

Maybe part of me still longs for the chance to see where Charles and I could take our relationship, provided he's willing to ditch his annoying realtor girlfriend. Or maybe I don't want to leave Bethany behind when we've worked so hard to overcome our differences.

It's also likely that I'm afraid of spending all day and all night at home with my crabby tabby for company. Nan lives with us now, too, but Octo-Cat reserves all his whining just for me. I mean, I guess it makes sense, seeing as I'm the one who understands him.

At the end of the day, life sometimes requires hard decisions.

Historically, I'm not so great at making them.

If I just give it a few more weeks, maybe the

right answer will fall into my lap. Yeah, I like that idea.

Until that happens, though, I'll just continue to wait and pray I get the courage to ask for what I really need. First, I'll have to make sure it's actually what I want, and then…

Watch out, world! I'm Angie Russo, and I'm coming for you.

"I come bearing muffins!" I cried as I bounded into the firm ten minutes late that morning. I still had a hard time calculating my new commute, but I hoped that Nan's homemade baked goods would more than make up for my tardiness.

"Ahem," somebody cleared his throat from the desk near the door. *My* desk.

I whipped around so fast, I fumbled my beautiful basket of muffins and dropped them straight onto the floor. All of Nan's hard work was ruined in an instant. It was a good thing she enjoyed baking so much and probably already had another fresh batch ready and waiting at home.

"Let me help you," the stranger said, rushing over to offer assistance I most definitely didn't need.

I watched him from the corner of my eye, still refusing to acknowledge this interloper's presence. From what I could discern, he was tall and gangly, with white-blond hair and thick, emo glasses.

"Oh, good," Bethany said, clasping her hands together as she strode toward us both with a smile. "You've met Peter."

"Peter?" I asked with a frown as the new guy stuck his hand out toward me in greeting. Looking at him straight on now, I saw he wore his dress shirt open with a t-shirt underneath that read *Awake? Yes. Ready to do this? Ha, ha, ha!* Charming. The disturbing top half was paired with wrinkly cargo khakis on bottom. Fulton and Thompson *never* would have let this fly in their days. Yeah, I knew the firm was mostly better off without them, but still couldn't we at least try to look like professionals here?

"You're Angie, right?" Peter asked, grabbing one of the muffins that had touched the floor and shoving it into his mouth with wide eyes. *"Mmm,"* he said pointing at it. "So good."

I disliked this guy more and more by the moment, but Bethany seemed so excited to introduce us that I forced a smile and shook his hand despite my better judgement.

"Peter's our new intern," she explained. "He's going to help you manage your workload."

"I don't need help managing my workload," I shot back, recoiling from Peter's grasp when he wouldn't let my hand go after the normal, polite period of time for a greeting.

Bethany frowned. "Not exactly true. It's been harder for all of us since you switched to part-time, but it's okay, because Peter is the perfect person to step in and smooth things out."

Yeah, me going part-time was the problem, and not the revolving door of partners we'd seen so far this year.

"What exactly are his qualifications?" I asked, regarding him coldly.

Peter popped the remains of that precious blueberry muffin into his mouth and mumbled, "I'm her cousin, and I work for minimum wage."

Bethany shot him a dirty look, finally showing me that he bugged her, too. That at least made me feel a little better about all this. "Really, Peter. You need to stop being so liberal about sharing your salary."

"Sorry," he muttered with a shrug that suggested he really couldn't care less about it.

Why was he here? I may not be the best paralegal in the world, but I was miles better than this guy. He probably didn't even have his degree. This was all wrong. I couldn't quite say why exactly, only that I hated everything about this Peter guy.

"Wait," I said, realizing something. "Your name is Peter Peters? You sound like a super hero."

"Or a super villain," he countered with another shrug and a strange, new smile.

"Anyway," Bethany said, glancing at her feet to make sure no errant muffin crumbs had attached themselves to her shiny patent pumps. "This is Peter's first day, which is why I asked him to come in a bit early. Can you help get him set up? Show him the ropes?"

"What kind of ropes?" I demanded. I didn't normally start my work day by playing babysitter to some annoying nepotistic hire.

No, right now, I was supposed to be in Bethany's office while she safely brewed me a cup of delicious, life-saving coffee. There was no way I'd touch another coffee maker as long as I lived, but I still enjoyed the extra jolt it gave me when someone else was willing to brave the brew master.

"Just the stuff you normally do," Bethany answered with a dismissive gesture, already turning to take her leave. "If either of you need me,

I'll be in my office. I have client meetings most of the morning, but should be free around lunch time."

"Okay, bye," I said, turning to my new charge, resigned that I would have pretty much the worst work half-day ever.

He smiled after his cousin. "Too-da-loo!" he called, waggling his fingers, then turned to me. "Okay, so I'm ready to learn how to be you when I grow up," he announced.

He did not just say that!

Well, so much for turning in my notice. There was no way I could leave the firm with this bumbling oaf of a paralegal. If only we could cue a makeover montage in real life. I'd choose one of my favorite upbeat 80's pop jams, spend a few minutes reforming him, then call it done and move on. Real life never worked fast enough.

"Let's go set up your email," I said with a sigh, leading him back to my desk that we now seemed to be expected to share.

"Cool, cool. And when do I get my company-issued iPhone?" He bobbed his head, following after me like a lost little duckling.

"What? Why would we give you an iPhone?"

"Uh, hello. FaceTime." He twisted his hands

and formed a rectangle about the size of a smartphone then looked at me through the gap.

And just like that, he went from simply irritating to downright terrifying. FaceTime was the same app I used to call my cat from work. Our senior partner, Charles, had found out when he was still brand new to the firm and bribed me to help him defend a client. Was it just a coincidence that this Peter Peters had alluded to it now?

Or did he know something that could get us both into very big trouble?

Oh, I did not like this. I did not like it one bit.

2

Unfortunately, the day only got worse as it went on. Peter met me with snark, indifference, or outright creepiness at every turn and quickly proved that he had zero of the necessary experience to do this job—*my* job. In fact, Peter grated on my nerves so much that I decided to go right over Bethany's head and appeal to our senior partner, Charles Longfellow, III. Surely he would see that hiring this guy was the worst kind of mistake?

Of course, things between Charles and me continued to be quite complicated. To start, I kind of, sort of, may have had some unresolved romantic feelings for him. We'd become close friends in the months since he'd joined the firm. It had all started when he discovered my ability to speak with Octo-Cat and then blackmailed me in order to help his client, Brock Calhoun the, um... other guy I kind of, sort of, may have had a bit of a crush on these days.

Still, despite the slight blackmailing, Charles was a consummate professional. It's how he'd managed to rise through the ranks at the firm so fast, and it was why I trusted him to do the right thing when it came to Peter. After finding a spot where his calendar was open, I barged straight into his office—so upset that I forgot to knock.

Oh, I wish I would have taken a quick second to knock!

"Angie," he said with a start, then cleared his throat and straightened his tie. It was the same tie Nan had bought him as a housewarming gift a month or so back—dark red silk with an intricate white paw print pattern that somehow managed to look both classy and kitschy at the exact same time.

His girlfriend, Breanne, untangled herself from his arms and glanced over her shoulder with a smirk. Her bottle-red hair clashed with Charles's tie, and everything else about her clashed with the rest of him, too. Of all the people in Blueberry Bay, I still couldn't believe he'd chosen to date *her.*

They'd been wrapped around each other for months now, and I was beginning to suspect they may end up walking down an aisle before too long.

Granted, I hadn't known Charles much longer myself, but I still thought that he and I would have made a much better couple—a much more logical one, too. As each day passed, it looked less and less like I'd get my chance to find out what could be there. *Stupid Breanne.*

"I'll see you tonight. Okay, babe?" Charles said after several awkward moments passed between the three of us.

"I'll be waiting," Breanne gloated as she accepted his kiss, then sauntered past me, hips swinging. Have I mentioned how much I actively loathed her? Because it was a lot.

Charles sighed and sunk down into his leather desk chair. "What's up, Angie?"

"Sorry to interrupt," I answered, rubbing my index finger on my thumb to try and loosen a hang-nail I'd been fighting all morning. It was a bad habit of mine—a nervous habit. Seeing Charles and Breanne's disgusting canoodling had knocked the speech I'd prepared clear out of my brain.

Guess I would just be speaking from my heart.

I closed the door behind me, then came closer

and took a seat in one of the two visitor chairs angled across from his desk. "It's about the new person Bethany hired."

"Peter Peters?" Charles asked with a slight snort. "What about him?"

"I don't like him," I said plainly, hoping Charles would understand without me having to go into more detail. "And I don't want him here."

Charles sighed. "He didn't make the best first impression on me, either. But, unfortunately, we do need the help."

"Can't we find somebody else?" I whined, not caring how pathetic it made me sound. Charles needed to understand that this was so much more than bad first impressions.

Charles pinched his brow and fixed me with an exasperated stare. "People aren't exactly lining up to work here given, um... our recent history."

Oh, right. The small fact that the other partners continued to leave under less than savory circumstances. All the extra clout we'd picked up after our near-impossible win on the Calhoun case had quickly dropped by the wayside when...

Never mind, best to focus on our current problems instead of dwelling on the past.

"If we're really that spent, I could come back

full time for a while." I enunciated each word while keeping careful eye contact. "Just until we find someone better than Peter, I mean."

Charles shook his head again. "I wish I could, but Bethany is my partner. We make decisions together now. If you just give Peter a chance, I'm sure he'll grow on you."

I rose to my feet and put my hands palm down on his desk, then leaned in as close as I dared. I wanted to slap him and kiss him in equal measure. *Stupid Charles.*

"I think he knows about me. About what I can do." I widened my eyes, refusing to so much as even blink until I was sure he understood.

"About you and," He gulped before continuing. "Animals?" When I nodded, Charles leaned back and let out a slow breath. "Well, that's not good."

I straightened to my full height once more. Whether or not we had a romantic connection, Charles and I had always seen eye to eye. I knew he'd get it. I knew he'd find a way to protect me.

That is, until he said...

"But it's also not possible. I'm sure it's all in your head."

"All in my head?" I demanded, throwing a hand on each of my hips. "You can't be serious!"

He glanced toward the far corner of the room instead of looking at me. "What do you want me to do, Angie? Fire him based on a suspicion? One that has nothing to do with what we actually do here, by the way."

I threw myself into his line of his vision. I was not just some problem that could be ignored. I was a real person and had a problem that demanded a satisfactory conclusion. "Yes, that's exactly what I want you to do," I practically shouted.

He cleared his throat again and shifted his gaze toward his keyboard on the desk. "Sorry, that's something I just can't do. Not without a valid reason to let him go."

I crossed my arms over my chest defensively and charged back toward to door. There were many things I wanted to say and do—chief among them quitting on the spot—but I simply walked out without another word.

I had to stop fast to avoid running straight into Peter who stood right outside Charles's office door, munching on a granny smith apple. "Trying to get rid of me?" he asked with a neutral expression, keeping his eyes fixed on the fruit in his hand. "That doesn't seem very welcoming."

"Why are you here?" I asked with a deep scowl.

Peter crunched into the apple again, and a spray of juice hit me on the cheek. He reached up with his thumb to wipe it away, but I jerked out of reach.

After swallowing everything down, he smiled and said, "Why do you think I'm here? It's to get close to you, Angie. To uncover your secrets and expose them to the world."

I took a step back, panic settling in my chest like a lead weight. I could scarcely breathe, let alone say anything in response to *that*.

Peter closed the distance between us and set a heavy hand on my shoulder. A smile broke out across his face and then he laughed. "Whoa, you really need to learn how to relax. Did you honestly just buy that garbage?" He shook his head as if dealing with an imbecile. "I'm here to make some money and help out my cousin. Okay? I mean, seriously, Angie." He continued to laugh as he breezed his way past me back toward our shared desk.

I stood rooted to the spot as I watched him go. How much had Peter heard of my talk with Charles? And how much did he already know? Moreover, why?

And how?

If he was on to me, there had to be others as well. Maybe Peter was just some kind of henchman and the big bad had yet to reveal himself or his plan. I'd never hurt anyone, and I'd become much more careful when it came to concealing my strange ability.

If someone was on to me, then what could I possibly do to keep Octo-Cat and myself safe? And why would they ever want to hurt or scare us as Peter's mannerisms seemed to suggest?

Suddenly, it felt as if nowhere would be safe. That, even if I ran, there were people out there who knew, who would always know.

What was I going to do?

3

I couldn't escape the office fast enough that day. Physical distance, however, did little to calm my already frayed nerves. The whole drive home I kept looking over my shoulder, half expecting to see Peter following me in some kind of old junker. I knew I didn't have any real hard and fast proof, but still, something within me screamed that he was out to get me, that we were quickly headed somewhere bad.

Very, very bad.

Sure, he could have been some harmless and ordinary, run-of-the-mill weirdo whose goal was simply to score a few laughs at my expense. He totally could have been. And yet...

Ever since I'd gotten zapped by that old coffee

maker and woken up with the ability to speak to Octo-Cat, my intuition had also been dialed up to at least a nine. I'd been wrong about some things, of course, but that was mostly when I let my personal feelings cloud my judgment. Whenever I stopped and listened to that still small voice, it led me straight to the answer I needed.

And right about now, that tiny voice was practically hoarse from shouting *beware* over and over again the past several hours.

As much as I hated it, this wasn't just about Peter moving in on my job and messing things up at the office. This was about keeping those I loved safe—and that now included the tabby cat who'd entered my life and turned it upside down again and again. How could someone I'd only just met already know the one very private thing I hesitated to share with anybody?

How could Peter have possibly figured me out when so few people knew what I could do and most of them were related to me?

I mean, Charles knew, but despite my disappointment in his response today, I trusted him not to tell a soul. Did that mean someone else at work had figured things out? Sometimes I slipped up and talked to my cat around others, but most people wouldn't just jump to the conclusion that we could communicate with each other. The normal thing would be to assume I'd gone wicked crazy. That didn't bother me since most days I was halfway there already.

I turned onto the secluded driveway that led to my huge manor house in the woods. The summer sun hung high in the sky, and my gardens were in full, beautiful bloom. In a lot of ways my life was pretty perfect—giant estate, wonderful family, cool cat, and a monthly stipend from his trust fund. So, then, why couldn't I just let this thing with Peter go?

"You look like you've had a rough day," Nan said, greeting me at the door when I entered our shared home just in time for a freshly prepared lunch. She and Octo-Cat both waited for me right in the foyer whenever I came home from work. Nan usually had a kind word and a hug. Sometimes, a joke.

Octo-Cat generally had a complaint. Today, he stretched out his toes, showing off his impressive claws, and moaned, "The sun is not bright enough today. It's hard to keep my schedule when my warm spot disappears halfway through the morning."

I shrugged off his concern, especially considering the sky had felt just as bright as ever during my return commute. "Sorry, nothing I can do about that."

I'd long debated getting him a heat lamp, precisely because of how often I heard this particular complaint, but that kind of felt like rewarding bad behavior. Ah, who was I kidding? It was just a matter of time before I'd ultimately cave. Heck, maybe I'd get him one for Christmas. Today, however, I had other things to worry about.

I took a long, appreciative sniff as Nan and I headed for the kitchen. Ever since we'd moved in together a couple of months ago, she'd taken it upon herself to cook up three square meals per day, finding a passion for the culinary arts a bit late in life but not lacking an ounce of enthusiasm nor, thankfully, talent.

"French onion soup," Nan revealed with sparkling eyes, which seemed to grow as she made this revelation. "Have a seat and I'll bring it right out."

I wanted to help, to give her a bit of a break, but she always pushed me right out of the kitchen and told me to hold my horses before they galloped away without me.

"What's got you so down in the dumps?" she

asked, setting a steaming hot bowl before me, then returning to the kitchen to grab a second for herself. My nan always knew when something wasn't right. She had the gift of intuition, too, but I suspected that came more from being a mother than from a near-fatal run-in with a coffee maker or some other such mildly supernatural experience.

"They hired a new intern," I explained, pushing my spoon through the thick layer of perfectly melted cheese and allowing it to fill up with broth, then shoving it appreciatively into my mouth. *Mmm.* So good.

Nan smiled when she saw how much I enjoyed what she'd prepared. Rather than taking a bite herself, however, she folded her hands before her and said, "Well, I'm guessing we don't much care for this new person." That was another thing about my dear, sweet nan—she always took my side. She didn't even need to hear a single detail before she was ready to jump into the fray and fight for my honor. Heck, just a couple months ago, she'd hit a police officer multiple times for attempting to cuff me.

"We most definitely do not," I answered, preparing a second mouthful of gooey goodness, complete with onion and cheese this time. "Not only is he creepy, but I also think he knows about me. You know, about what I can do."

Nan shook her head and sucked air in through her teeth. "Well, that's not good. Not good at all." Finally, she dug into her soup, choosing to eat one of the broth-saturated croutons first.

"What are we going to do?" I asked after giving her a play-by-play of the awful day I'd had.

"That Charles deserves a good scolding," Nan said with a grimace. "After all we've been through together, he won't even stand up for what's right."

I shrugged and let my spoon clatter to the bottom of my bowl. "I don't know. Maybe I'm just being oversensitive about the entire situation."

"Hey, I didn't raise you to talk like that," Nan shouted so loud and so abruptly, it made me jump with surprise. "We don't discount or apologize for our feelings. We're not robots. Right?"

"Right," I agreed with a sigh. "Then what should I do about Peter Peters and all the weirdness?"

Octo-Cat hopped up onto the table and strode down the center line. As he did, loose hair floated off his body and a piece or two wound up in my soup. Guess that meant I was done.

"If I may," he said grandly, halting right in front

of me and gesturing to himself with a paw. "I believe I have the solution to this problem."

"He says he has an idea," I translated for Nan, who smiled and waited for more. She loved watching the two of us talk, even though she needed a bit of help understanding Octo-Cat's side of the conversation.

"Not *an* idea," he corrected with a huff. *"The* idea."

"Well, what is it?" I asked impatiently. Sometimes his dramatics could be adorable, but this wasn't one of those times. I was far too stressed to sit and watch a show. I needed real-world solutions here delivered in a real-time fashion.

"You need to pull a stray cat on this guy," my tabby said plainly.

This, of course, meant nothing to me. "Come again now. What?"

"A stray cat. Not that I've ever been stray." He shuddered and flicked his tail. "But I've seen enough of them to know their modus operandi. They're free agents—strays—and most want to stay that way. But a cat can get real sick of eating trash when Fancy Feast is an option, you know? So, sometimes they have to make their eyes big, raise their tails, and do the pretty meow when a human is nearby. It hurts inside to fake it with a human—that much, *I do know* from experience—but it's just a couple moments of cringiness to get a full belly of food. Get it?"

I thought about this for a moment, ignoring the fact that he'd probably just insulted me. His cat-based analogies often took me a bit of finagling to truly understand, but they often did offer good and surprisingly relevant advice. I recapped Octo-Cat's speech for Nan, who seemed to understand instantly without even awaiting the full translation.

She nodded her approval to Octo-Cat, then turned back to me with a newfound fierceness burning in her eyes. "*Operation: My Enemy is My Friend*'s an official go," she said in a low, husky voice that I assumed belonged to her tough guy persona.

Still, no matter how much I wanted to find out what Peter knew and, moreover, what he wanted, I wasn't sure I could find a way to fake nice with someone I already despised so much.

Despite Nan's Broadway past, I hadn't inherited even one iota of her acting talent. So then, how was I going to trick Peter into revealing his motives here?

4

I wish I would have been surprised when Nan showed up at my work the next day wearing an all-black satin gown and bolero jacket combo. She kind of looked like she was ready to attend an elegant society ball and then rob its hosts on her way out. She'd even done her makeup much more heavily than normal to match today's bold style. Yes, winged liner and a smoky eye currently topped off my grandmother's day-time look.

I knew she sometimes missed the glory days of singing, dancing, and acting her heart out on the Broadway stage, but sometimes she took her real day-to-day life in Blueberry Bay a bit far. I still fondly remembered how she'd donned a black and white checked bodysuit to accompany me to my driver's test, or how she wore a cap and gown of her own to my high school graduation. Her wardrobe probably stretched all the way to Narnia for all the crazy outfits she kept hidden away until they were needed.

Was I embarrassed? Nope, not one bit.

I loved my nan and was long past feeling the need to apologize for her eccentricities. They were just as much a part of her as her loving, generous heart, and I wouldn't trade either of those things for the world. Still, I did have to wonder what she had up her sleeve—or rather, her gloved arm—with this one.

"Hello, good people of Longfellow, Peters and Associates," Nan declared, strolling into the office like she owned the place. In her hands she clutched a sealed Pyrex dish, which she promptly uncovered to reveal freshly baked apple turnovers.

Of course—*apple* because I'd mentioned the creepy episode with Peter outside of Charles's office yesterday. What I couldn't tell was whether this whole display was meant as a power play or rather a way to ingratiate herself as part of our so-called *Operation: My Enemy is My Friend.*

With Nan, you just never knew what was going on inside that wonderfully whacky brain of hers.

"Hi, Nan," I said, rising from the small corner of the shared desk that I'd claimed as my own. "What are you doing here?"

Peter stayed seated but kept his eyes on us while offering up a cool, casual smile.

"Hello, dear." Nan gave me air kisses instead of a hug, further proving that she'd decided to play some kind of character role today. Even her voice sounded grander, surer, as it reached to the far edges of the room.

"Well, of course, you know how I'm planning that fabulous dinner party later this month. I'm testing out some gowns and some recipes ahead of time to lessen the burden of all the choices I'll have to make as we get closer to the big day." She paused and dipped her head, after tossing me a quick wink. "Now tell me. How do I look?"

She spun in a slow, graceful circle as if there was absolutely nothing for either of us to be embarrassed about. The thing that made her a great actress, I knew, was that she truly lived every single role. Granted, she was simply playing a farcical version of herself today, but that didn't stop her from owning it one hundred percent.

"You look beautiful," I said with a big smile. I may not have always agreed with her methods, but

I had to admit that no one even came close to the space Nan occupied in my heart.

"Thank you," she said primly. "And, now, how do these taste?" she added, shoving the open Pyrex dish into my face with a desperate, needy look.

I plucked one of the desserts from the top of the stack and took a nibble. "Absolutely delicious," I answered honestly after swallowing down the perfect mix of sweet and tart. Part of me wished she had discovered this newfound passion for baking when I was younger so I could've enjoyed these talents longer. My waistline thought differently, though. I'd already had to go up one pants size this month, and I was not keen to go up another.

Nan frowned and her voice dropped into a husky pout. "Oh, but you always say what I want to hear. I need an impartial opinion." She spun around again, this time searching the room as if she didn't know Peter was the only other person around.

"You there!" she called, erupting into a full, sparkling smile as her eyes landed on a watchful Peter. "Can I count on you to give me your honest opinion? There's a free dessert in it for you, if you agree."

Peter hopped to his feet and sauntered over to join us. "I was hoping you'd ask." Without waiting for any further invitation, he grabbed two pastries from the stack and ate them in giant, appreciative bites.

"So good," he smacked, his mouth still full. "You should definitely serve these at your party."

Nan frowned again. "But you haven't tried the other options. How do you know for sure that these are the best?"

Peter chuckled and took a third apple turnover. "If they're all this good, then you have nothing to worry about."

Nan placed one gloved hand on Peter's arm and the other on mine. "Oh, I know!" Her eyes sparkled with the promise of a new idea, even though I had no doubt she'd arrived at the firm with this exact script already written and memorized. "Would you mind stopping by later tonight to try some of the others and offer your expert opinion on which is best?"

Peter faltered as he shifted his weight from foot to foot. Today he wore a tight t-shirt that had a bowtie and shirt collar printed onto it. He'd paired this with dark wash jeans and what I guessed was unintentional bed head. "Oh, I don't know if—"

"Please?" Nan begged, casting a pathetic shrug his way. "This party is so important to me. It might be the last I ever get to throw before God takes me back to the great dinner party in the sky."

Wow, she went there. She really went there.

"Oh, well. Sure, okay," Peter answered with a puzzled gaze that he quickly transitioned into a smile. "It would be my pleasure."

Nan perked up instantly. "Lovely. See you tonight, dear. Six o'clock?"

This whole time they spoke, Peter simpered at Nan and studiously ignored me. So, he only hated me, it seemed. At least I knew Nan believed me about his antagonism, even if my colleagues didn't.

He nodded now and took another two treats for himself. "Sounds like a plan."

"Excellent," Nan declared, then pushed the glass dish at Peter. "Why don't you keep these to remember me by? Just don't spoil your appetite for tonight." She reached up and pinched his cheek, then to my horror made a kissy face before letting go.

"Well, my dear," she said, turning back my way. "This gown may look divine, but it doesn't quite have the movement I need for an entire evening spent wearing it. Back to the boutique it goes!"

I nodded dumbly.

She glanced over my shoulder toward Peter and

blew him one last kiss goodbye. "Now I must be off. Angie has the address. Toodles!" And just like that, Nan blew out of the office every bit as quickly as she'd entered.

I headed back to the desk while Peter slumped down into one of the thick armchairs in our waiting area, helping himself to yet another turnover. "That was weird," he said.

I shrugged. "That was Nan."

He studied the pastry in his hand, then widened his eyes and shoved it into his mouth. "She's fun. I like her."

I shot him a polite, fake smile, then tried to return my focus to work.

Peter, however, seemed in the mood for a chat. "It's really too bad you don't take after her," he informed me with a sigh. "We'd have a much better time at work if you did."

I pretended I hadn't heard him, but he kept talking anyway.

"You don't look much like her, either. Maybe you inherited something else from her. You know, besides personality and looks. Maybe some secret trait or talent. *Hmm?*" He chuckled and brushed his sticky fingers against his jeans. "I guess we'll find out tonight."

Indeed we would. Poor Peter had no idea he was walking straight into a trap. Nan may seem crazy on the surface, but she's the best sleuth I know. Her interrogation skills are also top-notch.

Not to mention, Octo-Cat and I would also be there and ready to pounce on even the slightest suspicion. It may have been easy for him to pick on me at work, but my house was my fortress and filled with everyone who loved me most. For all his faults, I knew Octo-Cat would also do whatever it took to protect me. Even all these months later, he still found new and terrifying ways to surprise me.

Peter Peters didn't stand a chance.

5

Nan put me to work the moment I stepped through the door. She tossed me an apron and declared me in charge of mixing batter and rolling dough, the two tasks that were the most difficult to mess up, I noticed.

"It's all hands on deck. Only five hours until go time, and we have to make our ruse look believable," she explained with a curt nod. She'd changed out of her black satin gown from earlier and was now wearing a dainty crushed velvet number patterned with Chinese dragons. She'd replaced her smoky eye with a shimmering gold shadow and had contoured her cheeks like a Kardashian.

"I expect you to dress up, too, my dear," she explained while studying my unassuming floral dress with its giant, oversized belt and large hoop earrings as if it was the worst outfit anyone on earth had ever cobbled together.

Octo-Cat laughed between licks of his paw. "Being a human can be the pits, huh? A cat would never..." His eyes grew comically wide as his words trailed into oblivion.

I followed his line of sight to where Nan had been rummaging through the junk drawer. She now held out a red bow tie as she moved toward Octo-Cat with a broad, reassuring smile that only seemed to heighten his discomfort. "You, too, young man. We must all look our best tonight."

Nan then proceeded to fasten the bowtie to his collar with skilled and gentle fingers, but she may as well have been strangling the cat, given his over-the-top reaction.

"I am tainted!" he cried, shaking and twitching and throwing himself against the tile floor repeatedly. "Don't you know? I was born with all the clothes I'll ever need. So why add this? It's even the same color as that wretched dot! That's just taking things too far."

He heaved a giant sigh and fell over on his side when Nan had finished. I had to admit, he looked rather dashing. I did not, however, admit that aloud, or else I'd end up with cat puke in my bed.

Instead, I simply covered my mouth and tittered softly against my hand.

Nan smiled at our tabby approvingly. "Very handsome," she said in a way that was reminiscent of how she'd talked to Peter at the office that morning.

Octo-Cat continued to shriek and toss himself around the kitchen, pausing only briefing to shake his head and whisper, "*Et tu,* Nan? I thought you loved me."

"Chin up. It could be worse," I told him as I continued stirring and stirring until my hand cramped from the vigorous, repetitive motion.

"I don't see how," my cat told me, rolling onto his back and wiggling back and forth in an ill-fated attempt to shimmy loose of his adornment.

"Well, for starters, you're going to have to spend time with Peter tonight. Peter's the worst," I explained with a shudder as I placed the bowl back on the counter and flexed my hand. I would definitely be getting Nan a stand mixer for the next gift-giving holiday. Sure, they cost a lot, but it would be worth it to save my hands, and hers, too.

Nan popped a tray into the oven, but we had so

many different dishes underway that I had no idea what was on it. "Now, Angie," she said, turning back toward me with a wagging finger. "If *Operation: My Enemy is My Friend* is to be a success, you need to commit to character."

"Hey, I never agreed to take on a character and, by the way, neither did he." I tilted my head toward Octo-Cat, who was too busy trying to find a way out of his collar to notice I'd just stuck up for him. *Figured.*

Nan tutted. "If you don't believe it, then how will our guest?" she asked, then grabbed my wrist and pulled me to attention. "It is an honor to have Peter with us tonight. We're friends, and as such, we tell each other things without hesitation."

"Like what he knows and how he found out?" I said drolly.

"Precisely," she said, punctuating the word by jabbing a dripping spatula at my apron. "But if you remain hostile, we won't get anywhere. Can you soften up a little so that we don't have to fall back on plan B please?"

"What's plan B?" I asked, biting my lip as I waited for the answer.

Nan let out a little laugh. "Well, we—"

"You know what? It doesn't matter," I interrupted. It would be easier if I didn't know too much ahead of time. I was a terrible actress, anyway. "I'm in. The sooner we figure out the deal with Peter, the sooner we can be done and rid of him."

"Now there's the sweet girl I raised," Nan said with a chuckle, returning to the other side of the kitchen to ice an enormous layered cake.

Octo-Cat flopped onto my feet, rubbing himself all over my socks until they practically changed color from all the shucked off fur. "I... can't... breathe," he exclaimed between gasps. "I think this is how I die!"

I bent down to pet him and slipped my fingers beneath his collar to make sure it wasn't suddenly too tight. "It's just for a little while," I assured him. "I promise we'll take it off the moment Peter leaves."

He sat up and swished his tail behind him as he thought. A scary smile stretched across his fuzzy little face. "So, if he were to leave sooner rather than later, I could have my freedom?"

I nodded emphatically. I had no idea how he intended to make that happen, but if agreeing meant he'd try to help tonight, then I was all for making a deal. "Yes, definitely. I don't want him around, either," I reminded my cat.

"Then our goals align." Octo-Cat returned to all four feet and blinked hard. "If you'll excuse me. I need to prepare."

I watched him trot away, then moved to wash my hands in the sink so I could get back to work. Nan didn't need to know about whatever Octo-Cat had planned. In reality, I didn't even know what he had planned, but I had no doubt it would be amusing—if not mortifying. It was starting to feel as if I didn't even need to do anything now that Nan and Octo-Cat both had grand plans of their own.

Once I'd done all I could to help in the kitchen, Nan ushered me upstairs and informed me that I would be wearing my red party dress with tiny white polka-dots that evening. Well, at least Octo-Cat and I would match for the upcoming festivities.

I bided my time, even going so far as painting my nails a shining ruby red, figuring that Nan would appreciate this small gesture of my commitment to the character. By the time I floated back down the stairs, Peter seemed to have just arrived. He stood inside the foyer with Nan, wearing the exact same outfit he'd had on earlier that day.

"Well, don't you look quite fetching," Nan said kindly as she studied the faux tux printed on his old

T-shirt. "I love the irony of that ensemble. So clever."

Peter raked a hand through his messy hair and gave her a boyish grin, charmed as anyone who found themselves the subject of Nan's attentions.

Octo-Cat came racing down the stairs as well, a glint of determination shining in his amber eyes. "This ends now," he ground out as he passed me.

He walked straight up to Peter and rubbed against his legs while purring. Next, he transitioned to his hind legs and pawed at Peter's knees. He didn't do that for anyone. *Not ever.* Man, he must have been really desperate to get rid of that bowtie. I'd definitely have to remember that trick the next time I needed to trick him into doing something.

"He likes you," Nan said with a wink. "Why don't you pick him up?"

"I'm really more of a dog person," Peter said hesitantly.

"A dog person?" Octo-Cat asked in horror. "*Blech.* Gag me with a spoon. But, yeah, I can smell that canine stink all over this one. Totally not surprised."

Peter flinched, then cracked his neck on either side. "Should we go try the desserts? After all, that is why you invited me. Right?"

"Yes, dear. Come along." Nan led him toward the dining room while Octo-Cat and I stayed behind in the foyer.

"Was it just me, or...?" I began but let my words trail off. He'd flinched in response to what Octo-Cat had said. I was sure of it, and yet... there was no way. It was far too crazy to be believed.

"He reacted to me," Octo-Cat agreed. "I thought so, too."

"It was probably just a fluke," I said, keeping my voice low so as not to be overheard by Nan and Peter in the next room.

"But if it wasn't..." Octo-Cat shook his head and took a deep breath. "Now I'm just as curious as you are. Something's off about this one, and I'm going to prove it. C'mon, Angela."

He trotted off and I trailed helplessly behind, wondering what my cat could possibly have planned now and also wondering if Peter might really be like me. Did he get zapped by that old coffee maker, too?

I desperately hoped I'd have the answer by the time the evening was through, because if this big production didn't work, we probably wouldn't get another chance.

Peter already seemed on guard that evening.

Had he finally realized that we might be on to him just as much as he was on to us? And if he didn't want to be found out, then why was he working so hard to push my buttons?

Was everything in my overworked imagination, or was my entire world about to change?

I honestly didn't know which option I preferred...

6

Nan looked utterly beguiling in her getup for that evening. She'd even woven jade chopsticks through her hair in a fancy upswept hairstyle that complemented her angular bone structure quite nicely.

She often wore Asian-inspired garments, preferring their smooth, flowing lines to the more rigid structure of traditionally Western clothing. Between her style choices and my predilection for all things eighties, we really did make quite the pair.

I preferred eighties fashion simply because it was great fun. Nan, on the other hand, had done a brief tour abroad during the Vietnam War—not as a soldier, but rather an entertainer—and she'd fallen in love with everything about that part of the world. She'd managed to visit Japan, China, and Thailand over the years, too, and was greatly looking forward to the day when I'd finally agree to accompany her for an extended visit of all her favorite places. As for me, I wanted to get to know myself a little better before I ventured so far from home. Luckily, I was getting closer and closer to accomplishing just that with each passing day.

As loathe as I was to admit it aloud, Octo-Cat had made a huge difference in my life and had been a huge part of my recent self-discovery. I had a feeling I'd done the same for him as well. That was the thing about the people you loved— sometimes they made you crazy, but they would always be there for you in a pinch.

And this thing with Peter was the pinchiest situation we'd encountered yet. With the murders we'd investigated together, we at least knew what we were dealing with, what we were looking for. But with Peter? We now had questions on top of questions. As afraid as I was to discover where the answers may lead us, at least the three of us were firmly in this together.

Nan waited until Peter and I were seated at the

table, then disappeared into the kitchen to plate up her sweet creations.

"Nice house," Peter remarked, twiddling his thumbs in front of him. "How'd someone like you manage something like this?"

"It's my house," Octo-Cat announced, jumping up onto the table and plopping his rear right in front of Peter. "And I don't think I want you in it."

"Don't mind him," I said, pretending that everything was as normal as could be. "He's just a bit suspicious of new visitors."

"Nice kitty," Peter said, reaching a hand toward the tabby.

"If you touch me, I bite you," Octo-Cat informed him with a low growl.

Peter instantly recoiled. Was it because of the growl or the words that preceded it? *Hmm.*

"Good human," Octo-Cat said in that condescending way I'd grown to love. "If you poke the tiger, you're going to lose some fingers. That's how the saying goes. Isn't it?" He tilted his head to the side and flicked his tail, keeping his unblinking eyes on Peter the whole time.

Peter laughed nervously. "So, Angie, how long have you been working at—?"

"Don't talk to her." Octo-Cat hopped back onto his feet and stared Peter down with his ears folded back against his head. "Talk to me. Who are you, and why are you such a jerk? *Huh,* big guy? You think it's nice to pick on my human?"

Peter leaned back as far as he could in his chair and looked toward me with large, pleading eyes. "Um, could we maybe put your cat somewhere while I'm here? I think I might be allergic."

"More like afraid," Octo-Cat said, then punctuated it with his signature evil laugh. I'd never seen Peter so shaken. Granted, I hadn't known him very long, but still, it really did seem as if he could understand what my cat was saying to him.

"Oh, don't worry about him. He's harmless," I said with a dismissive shrug.

Octo-Cat growled again. "Oh, she has no idea just how harmful I can be," he told Peter with a low rumble.

"Who's ready for some heavenly confections?" Nan sang as she floated back into the dining room with an artfully arranged silver serving platter, completely unaware of what Octo-Cat had been up to during her brief absence.

I widened my eyes as I moved them between

Nan and the cat, trying to let her know that this was his show, but she didn't seem to get the hint.

"Bon appétit!" she cried, setting the tray between Peter and me.

"This looks amazing." Peter wasted no time in grabbing a rich puff pastry dessert and shoving it eagerly into his mouth.

"You want to know what's really amazing?" Octo-Cat asked, keeping his eyes trained on Peter. "My jokes. Seriously, I dare you not to laugh."

I selected a mini cheesecake bite for myself and smiled as I waited to see what would happen next. Octo-Cat's jokes were generally pretty terrible, but Peter didn't strike me as the type with a sophisticated sense of humor anyway.

"Okay, get this." Octo-Cat sat again, coming right up to the edge of the table so that Peter had to scoot back to avoid touching him. "What do you call a dog with a brain? Anyone? Anyone?" He paused and looked around. "No, nobody knows. Okay, I'll tell you—*a cat!*" He whooped and laughed hysterically while Peter attempted to make small talk with Nan.

I watched the whole thing in quiet fascination, smiling to myself as Peter struggled to maintain his composure. He certainly didn't enjoy getting a taste of his own medicine, the poor baby.

Octo-Cat yawned. "That one didn't get you. *Hmm,* okay. Well, I have lots more." He waited for Peter to take another bite before asking, "What's the difference between cat puke and a dog?"

Peter seemed to choke a little but recovered quickly.

"One's a slimy pile of disgusting excrement, and the other's cat puke. *Ha!*" Octo-Cat flopped over on his side and rubbed his back on the dining room table the same way he often did in the freshly cut grass outside. This was him luxuriating in the moment. He seemed to love taunting someone who deserved it.

I chuckled quietly, eliciting glances from both Nan and Peter.

"Everything okay, dear?" Nan asked, stopping the small talk she'd been making with Peter. I'd been so focused on the tabby's antics, I didn't even have the faintest idea what they'd been talking about.

"Yes," I answered quickly. "I just think it's funny how Octo-Cat invited himself along to the party. He seems to be really taken with you, Peter."

"Yeah, well." He cracked each of his knuckles and looked away.

"Tough crowd," Octo-Cat spat, pacing the length of the table once more. "Good thing I saved the best for last. Okay, who here knows why dogs can't tell jokes? No one? It's because they lose their minds whenever someone says *knock, knock!*"

At this, Peter snorted and then, at last, broke out into a full-fledged laugh. *Gotcha.*

I jumped to my feet and pointed at him. "I knew it! I knew you could understand him!"

Peter blanched and fumbled the dessert he'd been holding. "I don't know what you're talking about—"

"Oh, can it, honey!" Nan shot in. "The jig is up." I was pretty sure Nan didn't know what we were talking about, but it felt nice to have another ally on my side. She stood, too, and together we glared at Peter.

"Who are you, and why are you here?" I demanded.

"You invited me," he sputtered in equal parts confusion and irritation. "But if I'm not welcome anymore, I'll just go." He pushed his chair back and sped toward the door, but Octo-Cat leapt after him and sunk his claws into Peter's shoulder, hanging on for dear life as the lanky man tried to fight him off.

"Ow, what the…?" Peter cried as he spun and shook, but still Octo-Cat refused to let go.

"Say you can hear me," the cat hissed viciously. "Admit you understand."

When Peter said nothing, Octo-Cat sunk his claws in even deeper. Telltale droplets of blood appeared on his neck and dampened his shirt.

"Ouch! Fine!" Peter shouted. "I understand you. Now let go."

Octo-Cat hopped down and raced over to Nan, who'd taken a seat on our old Victorian couch while she watched this entire scene unfold. "Now that's the spirit," she told Peter. "And here I was afraid we'd have to tie you up before you'd willingly confess a thing."

"What do you want from me?" he asked, wiping at his wounds with a defeated scowl.

I crossed the room and stood before him with my arms folded over my chest. "What do *you* want from *me?* You're the one who started all this."

"I thought you might be like me," he explained in that whiny, nasally voice I'd come to hate over the last couple of days. "And, clearly, I was right."

I shook my head, refusing to admit anything. "So, why taunt me?"

"Why not? I was just having a little bit of fun."

"Need me to cut him again?" Octo-Cat asked, racing over to defend me.

Peter curled into himself defensively. "Please, no!"

"You need to tell me how you knew, and you need to do it now," I yelled, towering over him now.

Peter's voice came out muffled. "Or what? You'll sic your cat on me again?"

I tilted my head and smiled at Octo-Cat who bounced at my side, ready for more action.

"Actually, that's exactly what I'll do," I said, yanking Peter's arms away so that he'd look me in the eye again. "Now, are you going to talk or what?"

Peter shook his head. "Not here."

I nodded to Octo-Cat, and he took another step toward Peter. "You have the right to remain silent," he said. "And I have the right to defend the indefensible."

Indefensible? Ouch. I was pretty sure he was just quoting something he'd seen on his favorite TV show, *Law & Order,* but still.

"I'll talk. I will!" Peter cried. "I promise I will. It's just… it's not safe here, okay?"

Oh, Peter. How quickly he'd transformed from villain to victim.

"If not here, then where?" I demanded.

"If not today, then when? If not me, then who?" Nan chimed in, but was ignored by both of us.

Peter shoved his hand into his pocket and pulled out a black business card printed with silver lettering. "This is the address. I'll see you there Friday night. Around ten?"

"Fine," I said, yanking the card from him even though he seemed willing to give it freely. "And until then?"

"Just act normal at work. Not a word, I mean it." His eyes darkened for a moment, but he quickly shrugged it off. "So, if we understand each other, then I'm getting the heck out of here. Bye."

I watched in silence as he charged out of the house and sped off into the night.

"Well, that was interesting," Nan said after emitting a low whistle.

"Did you translate my jokes for her? They were some of my best yet," Octo-Cat said with another chuckle.

I just shook my head and wondered what Friday night would bring. I'd never met someone else like me, and frankly, I hated that the first other of my kind had to be someone as vile as Peter Peters. But now I was one step closer to figuring out why I could talk to animals, and maybe if I learned more, I could use my abilities more effectively. I could talk to more animals. I could solve more crimes.

Could Peter really have the answers I'd been looking for all this time?

Well, I'd know soon enough.

7

Friday couldn't come fast enough. Now that I knew there might actually be answers, I needed to hear them. My poor, tired mind was in overdrive trying to anticipate what Peter would say when we finally got the chance to talk things out.

Why could I talk to Octo-Cat and only Octo-Cat?

How could a quick zap from a faulty coffee maker land me with paranormal powers when the rest of the world carried on just the same as ever?

And how did Peter Peters factor into all of this?

I looked up the address he'd given me on Google Earth. It belonged to a squat brick building right in the heart of Glendale's tiny downtown area. Despite having lived in the area for my entire life, I'd never noticed that building before. Perhaps my eyes had always been drawn to the more colorful, vibrant storefronts, or maybe it was new.

I even drove past one day in search of clues and was disheartened to see a FOR LEASE sign taped inside the darkened window.

Right before I left work Friday, Peter pressed a folded-up Post-it note into my palm without offering a single word about it. I tried to act naturally, but the tiny yellow paper felt like it was burning a hole right through my flesh. Once tucked safely inside my car with the doors locked, I unfolded the note and read the single word that was written there: *Claw.*

Well, that made absolutely zero sense. I took a picture with my phone and texted it to Nan. *Peter just gave this to me. Any idea what it means?* I asked.

I waited for a few minutes. When her reply still hadn't come, I tossed the Post-it on my passenger seat and started my journey home. Nan often forgot her phone in various parts of the house and didn't realize it was missing until hours later. I could just ask for her feedback in person. After all, I'd be there soon enough.

At the stoplight, I glanced toward the note

again. Maybe the trick was in how the word had been written rather than in what it said.

Only the note wasn't waiting on the passenger seat where I'd left it.

I did a quick scan of the floor, assuming it had fallen. *No.*

I groped under the seat, but the light turned green and the car behind me honked impatiently, forcing me to return my focus to the road.

The remaining minutes of my drive were grueling. Peter's note had to be somewhere. It just had to be. I needed to look harder to find it. It's not like it could have disappeared into thin air.

Then again, I was now living in a world where it was possible for at least two separate people to talk to animals. My reality had already warped and stretched into a vaguely unrecognizable shape. So, then, why couldn't a tiny piece of paper go poof when no one was looking?

Correction: when *I* hadn't been looking. Suddenly, I felt as if a million invisible eyes were staring directly at me, that I was the only one who didn't understand what had happened.

Paranoid. Vulnerable. But not crazy.

At home, I frantically searched the car. Still nothing.

I couldn't believe that Peter was making me wait until ten that night. Why had he even made me wait at all? Was this some kind of trick? Why hadn't I suspected so earlier?

Gullible. Naïve.

Nan found me less than half an hour into my search. "Lunch is getting cold. Granted, the cold cuts were already cold, but..." She stopped halfway down the porch steps and cocked her head to the side. "What are you doing, dear?"

"Looking for something," I mumbled, sweeping my hand beneath the seat for the one-millionth time. "Did you get my text?"

"What text?" she asked in obvious confusion.

I sighed. "Nan, you really need to start keeping your phone on you. What if there was an emergency and I couldn't reach you?"

Nan skipped down the rest of the steps and thrust her phone in my face. "You mean this old thing? Hasn't left my side all day."

I yanked it away from her and entered the top-secret passcode, *1-2-3-4.* That was probably another thing I should talk to her about when this whole business with Peter was put to rest. "Look, I sent you a picture of..."

I opened her recent texts and saw the conversation we'd had a couple days ago, but nothing since then. The text had sent, right?

"Dear, you don't look so good. Come inside and have something to eat," Nan suggested, as was her way.

But I was a woman on a mission. I brought my phone back out and checked my texts, checked my photo stream, checked the Cloud even.

Any indication that the Post-It note had ever existed had now also vanished into thin air. Why? It just said a single word with no context. It's not like it was something dangerous.

Wait, what *was* that word again?

It seemed that knowledge, too, had been plucked straight from my brain. I wanted to throw up as the realization hit me.

Nan put a gentle hand on my back and guided me into the house. "Eat," she commanded after pulling out my chair and pushing me down into it.

I did my best, but I just couldn't stop thinking about the note, about Peter, about everything. I couldn't wait any longer for answers. I needed to go now and hope that someone would be around who could explain all of this to me.

"I'm just going to go run a quick errand," I told

Nan, not wanting to put her at risk in case we were dealing with something dangerous here.

Octo-Cat, according to his rigorously kept schedule, was now napping in the west wing of the house. That meant I could slip away without having to first explain to him why I preferred he not come.

Seizing my chance, I booked it downtown to the place I'd been fixated on all week. I hadn't tried to enter before, but now I found parking down the block and marched straight up to the presumably vacant building. A polite knock on the front door produced no results, nor did the frantic pounding that followed. I tried to peer in through the window, but everything appeared empty, dusty, uninhabited.

Was Peter just yanking my chain?

Sending me on a wild goose chase rather than giving me any real answers?

But then why the note?

It had seemed he wanted me to know about his ability—or at least to know that he knew about mine—but why?

I groaned in frustration and kicked the edge of the building.

"Come now, Angela. Try to control yourself," Octo-Cat said, appearing at my feet as if from nowhere. He yawned, then swiped a paw across his forehead.

"Where did you come from?" I asked, shaking my head in disbelief.

He looked bored with me already. "The car. Same as you."

No, something didn't make sense here. "We've never had a drive where you haven't clawed the heck out of my lap," I argued, crossing my arms over my chest and glaring at him. "How could you have possibly stowed away undetected?"

He shrugged his little striped shoulders. "You're improving your skills. I'm improving mine."

"Well, that's just great." And, under normal circumstances, it probably would have been, but I was too frustrated about all the non-answers floating around when it came to Peter, his Post-It, and now this building, too.

I pulled on the door handle, but it didn't budge. With another massive groan, I slapped the edge of the building and bit back a scream. Now my hand and my foot hurt from abusing this stupid brick façade, yet I was no closer to figuring things out than I had been before stupid Peter came to stupid town. Grrr.

Octo-Cat lay on the sidewalk with his face

hidden beneath both paws. “You’re embarrassing me,” he ground out.

Great, great, great. I threw my hands up and charged down the block, back toward my car.

“Wait!” he called after me, running a short distance and then stopping at the alley. “We can still check the other sides, right?”

Darn it, he was right. I took a deep breath, then turned back his way.

Down the alley there was only a single door partially obscured by an overflowing dumpster. I lifted my hand and made a fist, but then hesitated. What would I find inside? Once I knew the truth, there would be no going back. Was I ready for that? *Really* ready?

“Well, go ahead and get it over with already,” Octo-Cat said gently.

I knocked so lightly, the sound barely even reached my own ears.

But a voice immediately answered from the other side. “Password?” it demanded.

Password? Peter hadn’t said anything about…

“Claw,” I said before my brain had even finished connecting the dots.

The door opened.

8

The man who opened the door was slight and gangly with a massive array of freckles scattered across his pale face. Definitely not the type one would expect to see in the role of security for...

What was this place?

I squinted my eyes and strained to see in the dank lighting. The inside looked very much the same as the outside—all brick and *blah.*

"Who sent you?" the bouncer asked, guiding us down the long staircase. His eyes shone a beautiful shade of green I'd never seen before—and not just in nature, but had truly never glimpsed under any context.

"Peter Peters," I muttered, searching the big,

empty space, but seeing nothing beyond the guard in front of me and Octo-Cat at my feet.

The guard shook his head and wrinkled his nose in a way that suggested perhaps he also didn't think much of Peter. "He's not due in until later tonight, but go ahead and have a seat if you want. You're welcome to have a drink while you wait."

I scanned the room again, wondering how I could have missed something as large as a bar in my previous glance about. "Um, where?" I asked nervously when I was still only met by dust and dirt and cobwebs.

The guard jabbed me in the ribs playfully, but it still hurt. "Ha ha, good one."

I let out an awkward laugh, truly not knowing what I should say next. Should I ask how he knew Peter, or would it be better to inquire about how the door had just magically appeared in the alleyway earlier?

"Who are you, and what is this place?" Octo-Cat asked the guard, shifting his weight from one side to the other, clearly unnerved by the filth of our current surroundings.

Our strange host answered him directly. "I'm Moss O'Malley. Haven't you ever been to the lair before?" If you're keeping count, that's now at least three of us who could talk to Octo-Cat. I definitely wasn't alone, not anymore.

"Can't say that we have," I answered for the both of us, pointing at my chest emphatically. "At least *I* haven't."

"Me neither," Octo-Cat supplied.

Moss stiffened. "You did say Peter sent you, right?"

We both nodded, eager to learn more.

"What would that dog want with you two?"

I ignored Moss's strange choice of words and also the fact that he seemed to be edging back toward the stairs.

"That's personal, I—" I began.

"Clearly she can talk to animals, doofus," my very unhelpful tabby interjected. He lived by one simple motto: *when in doubt, add an insult.* That didn't seem to be a good plan right about now. We were both in over our heads with Moss and his strange lair here.

Moss's attention shot back toward me, and he sniffed. "But you don't see the bar over there?" He pointed a shaking finger toward the far corner of the room.

I followed with my eyes, but still saw nothing

beyond the empty, dirty basement. "Well—" I began.

But before I could come up with a good excuse, Moss pushed me back up the stairs with surprising strength. "Just forget you ever saw this place, okay?" he said after tossing both me and Octo-Cat into the alley. Next he did something strange with the fingers on one hand and then slammed the door shut before either of us could demand an explanation.

Octo-Cat twitched and flicked his tail. "That fool manhandled me. My precious coat is a mess!"

"What just happened?" I asked breathlessly, watching in disbelief as the outline of the door faded into the brick wall right before my eyes.

"A little help here?" Octo-Cat cried, and I crouched down to help straighten his fur.

"He... he scruffed me," my poor cat sputtered in tears. "Scruffed me!"

"I'm so sorry," I whispered, glancing back toward the door but finding that same unforgiving swatch of bricks where it had once been.

"Can we..." Octo-Cat let his words trail off and then sighed heavily. "Can we just head home? I need to be in my own environment for a while."

I still didn't know what had just happened.

Would it have been different if we'd waited until ten like Peter had asked?

It was tough to say. We may have gotten more answers, but we also might have gotten ambushed. Moss hadn't told us much, but he'd made it clear that he also didn't much care for Peter. Maybe we should initiate *Operation: the Enemy of my Enemy is my Friend*. If Nan was here, that's surely what she would suggest.

But how could I get more out of Moss when I had no way of reaching him again? If I came back tomorrow, might I find the door again? Would Moss let me back inside? Or might a different guard welcome us to the lair? Would I be able to pretend I knew and saw everything?

Neither of us said a word on the short drive back home. As soon as I dropped Octo-Cat off at the manor house, I headed back into town to do some more reconnaissance on the mysterious underground lair. On my first drive through downtown, I accidentally passed it and had to turn around and track back.

It seemed a pretty silly mistake, one I'd probably made due to the fact my mind was still reeling from the earlier encounter with Moss.

I willed my brain to be quiet and focused hard, but still, I somehow managed to pass by it again.

Frustrated, I parked my car on the street in a sloppy parallel job, then went to search on foot.

An hour passed.

Two.

And still I could not find the lair again.

"I'm not crazy," I muttered to myself. "I'm not."

I checked in at home for dinner, then came straight back to town so that I could wait nearby for Peter. He said he'd be here at ten, that we could talk, and—most importantly—that he'd have answers.

People passed me on the street, shooting questioning glances my way, but I didn't care. I needed to know what was going on with me, now more than ever.

Nine o'clock came. *Just one more hour to go.*

Nine thirty.

Nine forty-five.

Ten came and went with no sign of Peter.

At five after, police sirens erupted in the quiet night. They grew louder and louder until the red and blue flashing lights were right upon me.

For a moment, I worried that I was about to be arrested for loitering, but the cop car flew right past me and stopped a couple blocks away. Now I had a choice to make—continue to wait for Peter or go investigate.

With one longing glance back toward where the lair should have been, I put my head down and jogged down the street to meet Officer Bouchard as he climbed out of his police cruiser.

"What happened?" I cried, short of breath despite the fact I'd only jogged a couple blocks. If only I could be in as good of shape as Nan. Maybe when this was all said and done, I could ask about accompanying her to that Zumba class she was always raving about.

My friendly neighborhood policeman just shook his head. "Got called about a robbery in progress, but the door is still locked and there's no sign of forced entry."

I peered into the lit up storefront, an upscale bridal boutique that folks from all across Blueberry Bay visited when they were ready to tie the knot. Nobody was inside. "Where did the robber go?"

Officer Bouchard shook his head again and turned to me. "You're on foot. That means you were nearby, right? Did you see anyone? Anyone at all?"

"No. Sorry." I frowned, wishing I had a different answer for him.

The officer let out a frustrated sigh and raked a hand through his overgrown hair. “Third time this week we’ve had a call like this. The security tapes always show up empty, but sure enough, the registers and safes are cleaned out. I’d say it was all for show—you know, insurance fraud—but it keeps happening. For the life of me, I can’t figure out how.”

I sucked in a shaky breath, choosing to keep quiet even though I had a sneaking suspicion the lair might somehow be involved with all of this.

I was well past beginning to suspect I wasn’t the only one in Glendale with a super power. Yes, Peter I already knew about, but how many others stood hidden in plain sight as they went about their daily lives? My talking to animals was innocent enough, but what could others do? Could they make whole buildings disappear? Commit a burglary without leaving a trace? Murder someone without ever being suspected?

I gulped down the giant lump that had formed in my throat. “I’m sure there’s a perfectly logical explanation,” I told Officer Bouchard, praying my words would prove true, but also knowing that they wouldn’t.

They couldn't. We were so past normal at this point, we weren't even in the same zip code.

Octo-Cat and I had taken on murderers more than once, but those were just regular, everyday people. Bad people, absolutely. But still *regular.*

What would happen when we found this mysterious new breed of magical criminal?

We wouldn't stand a chance...

9

Over the weekend, I spent some time reading news articles and social media posts about the recent rash of burglaries in downtown Glendale. Sure enough, the reports matched up exactly with what Officer Bouchard had told me. I also cruised through downtown a few more times hoping to spot the lair or to run into Moss again. Of course, that plan failed spectacularly.

"Why are you so bothered about this?" Octo-Cat asked me when we snuggled into bed Sunday night. "The building vanished and the mean scruffer guy went with it. They're not here anymore and thus..." He paused for emphasis and licked his chest. "Not our problem."

Maybe my cat didn't think all these strange goings-on were his problem, but I definitely considered them mine. Nothing bad would happen to him if people found out I could talk to him. I was the one in possible danger here, and it hurt that this failed to concern him.

Rather than sharing my hurt feelings, I decided to take a different approach to get him back on my side. "Aren't you at least a little bit curious about how a whole building could just up and vanish like that? Don't you want to know what happened?"

Octo-Cat lifted a leg over his head and began to lick parts that would be better tended to in private. "Curiosity killed the cat," he mumbled by rote. "And seeing as I only have five lives left, I'd rather not take too many chances."

It always weirded me out when he talked like this, and given Octo-Cat's flair for dramatics, it was hard for me to tell whether he was being serious or not. "Have you really died four times before?" I asked him quizzically. "I have a hard time believing that."

He lowered his leg, then stretched in a long arc with a satisfied mew. "It doesn't matter what you believe. All that matters is what's the truth. And whether you can do anything about it."

I contemplated this for a few moments. It seemed intelligent, even though it didn't satisfy my intense need to understand. "That makes sense," I said at last. "I know you're over it and everything, but do you have any idea what happened with the lair on Friday?"

"Sure I do." He rolled onto his back and wiggled around a bit. For all his complaints, he'd been doing a lot of that happy rolling about lately.

"Well," I demanded impatiently. "Are you going to keep it to yourself or will you just tell me already?"

He flopped back onto his side and twisted his mouth in a grimace. "I can tell you, but you're probably going to fight me on it."

"Why would I—"

"Magic," he said, cutting me off mid-sentence.

Well, that was a bit surprising, but not altogether unexpected, given recent events. "Magic? Could you maybe be more specific, please?"

"Mmm, no. Probably not." He yawned and offered me a little shrug. "I don't really know more than that."

Honestly, the fact he knew anything at all surprised me. Now that I knew he had at least some intel, I was dying to hear more. I had to play this carefully, though. If I got too excited, my cat would punish me by simply walking away from the conversation until I got a hold of myself.

"But you say magic was involved?" I asked without making eye contact as I dragged my fingers across the soft comforter on my lap. "Does that mean you believe in magic?"

"Please refer back to my previous statement about belief versus truth," Octo-Cat answered drolly, then waited while counting under his breath. Was he actually giving me time to revisit our earlier conversation? His arrogance truly knew no bounds.

"Okay," I said, trying to hide my annoyance. "Please continue."

He nodded appreciatively. "Thank you. And, yes, magic *is* real. Although it's also very rare. And before you can ask, I know because some cats can see the traces it leaves behind. Not me, mind you. Just some other, less cool cats."

Unbelievable. I shook my head and suppressed a sigh. "So this whole time you've known magic is real and you've never said anything to me? You can spend hours telling me about your napping routine, but never once thought to mention magic?"

Octo-Cat stood up and arched his back defensively. "If you'll recall, I mentioned magic on our very first meeting. Back when you were still trying to figure out how we can talk to each other. You told me there's no such thing as magic, and so I dropped it."

I thought back to that day so many months ago, and... *he was right!* He was absolutely, unmistakably right. But he'd never been one to drop anything, so why would he have let something so important slip away?

Octo-Cat's golden eyes glinted as he studied me. "I know what you're thinking, and the answer is *no.* I don't think you should mess with this more than you already have. I've already gotten scruffed once. What further proof do you need that these guys don't play fair?"

"Am I...?" I hesitated. This was a hard question to ask, a hard possibility to come to grips with. "Am I like them?" I asked at last, my voice shaking.

Octo-Cat rolled over on the bed and laughed heartily. "Like them? What do you mean by that? Do you think you're some kind of wicked witch now just because you can talk to the great Octavius Maxwell Ricardo Edmund Frederick Fulton Russo? Mind you, that's no small thing, but..." He broke apart in full-on laughter, rolling from side to side in glee.

My patience had more than grown thin by now. Once again, my cat had important information, information that I needed to solve a case. Yes, once again, he was being a brat about sharing it with me.

Finally, he sobered enough to say, "There's no such thing as witches or wizards, so drop those fictional stereotypes from your mind. Mmm'kay?"

"But—"

"But there *is* magic," he stated again. "I don't know much more, because I'm not someone who has any."

I pointed to myself, jaw hanging open. My lips simply couldn't form the words.

Octo-Cat shook his head. Magic or not, he clearly understood me. "And neither are you. Yeah, somebody's magical residue probably rubbed off on you or something. Hey, try not to look a gift cat in the mouth."

"So, what do I do?" I sputtered. My cat had just revealed a whole new hidden world, and my brain was racing a thousand miles an hour to keep up.

Magic was real. Who'd have ever guessed it? Certainly not me.

"You? *You* do nothing. Me? *I* do nothing. Just

forget we had this talk, okay?" He jumped off the bed and left the room, thus ending the conversation. Why was he being so cagey? Did he know more than he was letting on? Would he be willing to talk if I tried bringing up the topic later?

Unfortunately, you just never knew when it came to Octo-Cat.

My only hope now was that Peter would be more forthcoming when I approached him tomorrow at work.

* * *

Peter beat me to the office the next morning and appeared deeply involved with something on his computer screen when I entered.

"Hey," I said halfheartedly by way of good morning. Something told me I'd do best to approach him like I would Octo-Cat. *Carefully.*

"Hey," he mumbled back without so much as a glance my way.

"What happened Friday night?" I asked casually as I made my way toward our desk.

Peter burst out of his chair and clapped a hand over my mouth, scaring the wits out of me in the process. “Don’t,” he warned before peeling back his fingers one by one. “Just don’t.”

“But I waited for you,” I argued with a steely gaze. He could act weird all he wanted, but I wasn’t going to be frightened off—at least not until I finally got the answers he’d been keeping just out of my reach.

He shrugged, returning to his normal disinterested affectations. “Yeah, well, something better came up.”

“Okay,” I said slowly, pausing to take a slow, shuddering breath. If I lost my cool, we’d get nowhere. Whatever game Peter was playing, I needed to play it, too. “Can we try again some other time?” I asked sweetly.

“Stop acting like a scorned lover,” he spat. “It isn’t flattering.”

“But—”

Peter raised his hand and made the same odd gesture that the bouncer at the lair had made just before the door disappeared. I watched, mesmerized.

It made me feel happy—no, not happy, *content.*

Good.

Satisfied.

Ahh.

Someone cleared her throat from across the room, and I turned toward Bethany with a goofy smile planted on my face.

"Angie, a word in my office, please?" Despite the kindness of her words, she did not sound happy. Didn't look it, either.

"What's going on with Peter?" she demanded after I'd eased the door shut behind me.

I shrugged. My body still felt light, my mind fuzzy. It took me a little bit to come up with an answer.

Then I remembered.

Peter. I hated that guy.

"He's annoying, and I wish you hadn't hired him," I said with a scowl. All my earlier elation was now gone.

Bethany regarded me suspiciously from behind her desk. "Anything else?"

This was it. Someone was finally willing to listen to my misgivings when it came to Peter Peters. Only I couldn't exactly remember what they were.

Bethany tapped her fingers on the desk and raised one perfectly groomed eyebrow. "Well?"

"Nothing specific," I said, wondering why it

seemed all my recent memories had fallen clear out of my brain. "I just don't like him."

A smile washed across her face, replacing the anxiety that had been there only seconds earlier. "Good," she said, and then, "Thank you, Angie. That will be all."

I had no idea what was going on or why the conversation bothered me so much. Why did my head still feel like it was full of cotton?

Maybe I was coming down with some kind of cold.

Or maybe Peter…

No.

No way.

I felt like the answer lay just along the edges of my mind, but no matter how I strained, I couldn't break through the barrier to retrieve it.

Maybe the inevitable had finally occurred.

After months of talking to my cat, I'd now completely lost my mind once and for all.

10

"How was Peter today?" Octo-Cat asked over lunch. Normally he slept straight through our afternoon meal, but today Nan had prepared a tiny saucer of clam chowder for him, too, so that he could join us at the table.

My day up until that point had been completely unremarkable, which made it all the more unnerving that my cat seemed to expect me to share some wild, juicy gossip. "Fine," I answered slowly, still not knowing what else he expected me to say. "Why are you asking about Peter?"

Octo-Cat stopped lapping his soup and stared at me aghast. Droplets of cream clung to his fur, but he didn't seem to notice—or at least not to mind. "What do you mean *why?* Remember his visit here?

Our trip downtown to the lair? Any of that ringing a bell for you?"

"The lair..." That sounded familiar. Didn't I...? "Oh, right!" I shouted as it all came rushing back.

"What's the lair?" Nan asked from her spot at the head of the table.

"How could you forget?" Octo-Cat cried as he continued to study me with a worried expression. "It was seriously all you could talk about this weekend!"

I dipped my spoon into my soup and watched the steam rise before me. "Today was weird," I said at last. Then to Nan, "The lair is what was at the address Peter gave me. Or, at least it was, until it disappeared."

"And you were talking about it all weekend but didn't once mention it to me?" She seemed hurt and intrigued in equal measures. It wasn't easy to upset Nan, which meant I felt extra crummy whenever I managed to do so.

"I'm sorry. I didn't think it was safe, but I can't exactly remember why," I tried to explain, but kept coming up short.

"Wow, they really did a number on you," Octo-Cat said with a low growl. "I didn't think it was worth investigating, but if they're working this hard to mess with your memory, maybe it is."

My memory? Is that why my brain had been so fuzzy today? In a way it made sense, but people couldn't really just make someone forget—at least not outside the movies. "You think they wiped my memory?" I mumbled as Octo-Cat's eyes continued to bore into me.

"Uh, yeah!" he cried with an agitated swish of his tail.

"Who's they?" Nan asked gently.

I looked to Octo-Cat for the answer.

"Magic folk," he spat in disgust.

"Magic?" I asked with a start. Had we already discussed this? Was I again forgetting something important?

"Magic!" Nan shouted in delight. "Has magic finally come to Blueberry Bay?"

Now we both zeroed in on Nan. "You know about magic?" I squeaked. Had I been the only one in the dark here?

She laughed it off. "No, but I'd like to. It sounds fun."

"No," I snapped at her. "Please don't get involved in this one, Nan. I'm begging you."

She crossed her arms over her chest and stared me down. "Fun or not, where you go, I go. This time, it just so happens to be fun. Now catch me up."

Or really, really dangerous, I mentally added as my stomach did an impressive series of somersaults.

Octo-Cat guided me through the events of the past week, both to refresh my stolen memories and so that I could share with Nan. As he recounted each detail, I instantly remembered them in full. How strange that I hadn't been able to recall anything without his guidance.

"So," Nan said, rubbing her hands together as she prepared to sum things up. "Peter can talk to animals, too. There's a magic club downtown that can disappear at will, and someone is using magic to rob the shops downtown blind. Is that everything?"

"What do you mean is that everything?" I asked. Where earlier my brain had felt light and fuzzy, now it felt heavy from the burden of all this information slamming into it at once. "It's an awful lot all on its own."

Nan stood abruptly and headed toward the foyer.

"Where are you going?" I sputtered. *Dizzy.* I

needed to lie down, but I also couldn't let Nan walk into a dangerous situation all on her own.

Luckily, the next thing she said was, "We need to go shopping."

"What? Why?" I rubbed my temples to try to get the blood flowing to my brain again.

Nan appeared completely unbothered by this strange turn of events— rather, she appeared to be genuinely excited. "I don't have any good outfits for a stakeout, and I doubt you do, either."

"A stakeout?"

"Yes, that's what I said. Now, are you coming or what?"

Nan and I went to Target and bought new outfits, complete with nondescript black skull caps for each of us. She even bought Octo-Cat a tiny black bandana, which I knew for a fact he would despise.

The rest of that evening was spent baking and putting together a custom stakeout kit that included board games, blankets, audiobooks, and other random items meant to help pass the time. I mostly just tried to stay out of the way while Nan prepared for our upcoming adventure.

When night fell, she popped onto her feet, narrowed her gaze, and said, *"It's time."*

Honestly, between Nan's spy movie obsession and Octo-Cat's legal drama TV addiction, I was burnt out on this stakeout before it even began. Hopefully it would actually lead to some helpful new information—but I wasn't holding my breath.

"We'll take my car," Nan declared. Her little red sports car was less than discreet, but arguing would get me nowhere, seeing as she'd already committed to whatever role she planned to play tonight. Maybe a silver-haired female James Bond? I guess that made me the bimbo sidekick.

We parked downtown and sipped on matching thermoses filled with hot chocolate. Octo-Cat complained heartily from his place in the tiny, cramped backseat.

"Watch for anything suspicious," Nan instructed in a cautious whisper, even though no one was around to hear either of us. "Keep an eye out for anyone nosing around the lair or entering one of the shops after closing time," she further clarified.

"How long are we going to stay out here?" I asked with a yawn.

"As long as it takes," she answered, her jaw set with determination. "We can sleep in shifts if we have to."

Well, that didn't sound fun at all. Hopefully our

magical crooks would reveal themselves quickly so we could go home and snag a proper night's sleep.

Time passed slowly as Nan recounted the plots of all her favorite action flicks. Downtown Glendale slowly stilled as the businesses shut down for the night and people headed home. Other than the odd stray dog that galloped past, no one came or went. *Nothing happened.*

That is, until something did.

A clanging alarm sounded just down the street, and bright lights flooded the darkness. I recognized the jewelry store at once. Nan wasted no time reversing more than a half dozen parking spots bringing us to idle right in front the shop with the triggered security system. Despite the alarms and the lights, I couldn't see anyone inside.

Officer Bouchard showed up a few minutes later, sirens blaring just as they had Friday night. "You again," he said upon spotting me.

"It's a coincidence," I said, putting my hands up in mock surrender. "I promise."

"We were on a stakeout," Nan said, setting her mouth in a firm line.

"We just wanted to help," I said quickly. "See if we could catch the robber in action."

"And you brought your cat with you?" he asked, spying Octo-Cat through the open car window.

"I'm just really attached to him," I said between clenched teeth as Octo-Cat preened in my peripheral vision. "But I didn't see who broke in."

"The owner's on the way," Officer Bouchard explained. "But I think it's best that you clear out before he gets here."

Nan tapped her temple and smiled up at the handsome policeman. "Smart," she said. "We're the only witnesses, so naturally he'll suspect us."

I glanced back toward the lair and thought I saw a dark figure disappear around the alley. I wanted to go investigate but couldn't make Officer Bouchard any more suspicious of us than he already was.

As a compromise, I ducked my head back into the car and spoke in a low hush. "Octo-Cat, I saw someone or something by the lair," I whispered. "Can you go check it out?"

"On it," he said, sneaking out through the open window that faced the street.

"Thank you for your time, Officer," Nan cooed, shameless flirt that she was. "I know you're very busy and important, and it always feels nice when you take a little extra time out from your day for us."

"No more stakeouts," the cop called after her as he walked away. "You hear me?"

Nan gave a salute, then sank into the driver's seat.

I pressed the button to roll up the front windows and then whispered, "Stall for a few minutes. Octo-Cat is checking something out for us real quick."

Nan made a great show of fumbling her keys and taking inventory of the various supplies and activities she'd brought for our big stakeout. When at last Octo-Cat climbed back through the window, she gave a friendly wave and then peeled off into the night.

"What was it?" I asked my cat.

"Nothing," he said as if he still had a hard time believing it. "Absolutely nothing at all."

How could we have missed everything when it had happened right before our eyes?

It seemed the only thing our stakeout had accomplished is making me even more afraid of the magical forces that had taken hold of my hometown.

11

The next morning I woke up to Nan wearing a velour jogging suit with the word *sassy* written across her tush. A matching pink sweatband pushed her gray curls out of her face, and she held a metallic purple water bottle clutched firmly in one hand.

"The stakeout continues?" I asked, wiping the sleep from my eyes.

She stretched her arms overhead and then bent to touch her toes. "I'm sure I don't know what you're talking about," she answered with a wink while stretching both arms to one side and then the other. "I'm just headed into town to do a little exercise. Keeps me young and spry."

"Well, don't forget to take the cat with you," I

said, doing my best to hide the smirk that slithered its way across my face. "His harness is on one of the hooks in the laundry room."

I finished getting ready for work, and Nan and I had a quick breakfast together before saying goodbye. Octo-Cat, however, flatly refused to speak to me—the harness being one of the few things in this world he hated more than dogs. His irritation aside, Nan really did need his help on her investigation. A leashed-up cat might make her a bit of an inconspicuous character, but her snooping would have been obvious even without the cranky feline partner. At least now she'd have a second set of eyes and ears to help her out.

As for me? I had to go all by myself to face Peter yet again.

Fortunately I, too, had an operative planned for that day. It definitely wasn't like me to keep forgetting, so I grabbed the digital voice recorder Nan liked to use to record her monologues, popped in a pair of fresh batteries, and tucked the device into the corner of my bra. Once at work, I'd turn it on and record everything that happened that day. I mean, nobody could tamper with my evidence if they didn't know it was there, right?

God bless my giant boobs. Usually they were

just a pain in my back, but today they'd finally serve some kind of actual purpose. Maybe James Bond had more than one reason for keeping all those ample-bosomed sidekicks around, after all.

Whatever happened next, I was ready. We all were.

That morning, Peter arrived at the firm before I did, a fact that didn't quite feel consistent with the rest of his personality, now that I thought about it. I said hello, then slipped into the bathroom to power on my recorder.

"Did you have a good night?" I asked Peter conversationally when I returned to settle into our shared desk.

He groaned and shifted abruptly in his chair to face me. "I know you saw me, so cut the BS. What part of drop it don't you understand?"

"Drop what?" I asked casually. Meanwhile, my heart thrummed inside my chest. Was I close enough to the truth that he'd finally tell me what he knew?

Apparently not, because his expression grew venomous as he said, "Just back off, all right?"

I folded my arms across my chest in defiance and spun toward him in my twirly office chair. Our knees were less than an inch apart as I leaned even closer and captured Peter with my most determined glare.

"You're the one who pushed me first. Why would you do that if you didn't want to talk about...?" I paused for a brief moment before settling on, "Um, what we have in common."

He curled both hands into fists, and for a second there, I truly thought he might punch me. But then he sighed, released some of the tension, and whispered, "This is not the place to have this conversation."

I had him on edge. That had to count for something. Heck, maybe if I pushed a little harder, he'd teeter right over, yelling all his secrets on the way down.

I refused to let him intimidate me. Instead, I jabbed a finger in his chest and ground out, "Maybe not, but you stood me up last time we tried to meet somewhere else, and I'm done taking chances."

"I didn't stand you up," he practically shouted, then took a deep breath and worked hard to compose himself once more. "I didn't stand you up. You're the one who broke the deal by showing up early and bringing the cat with you."

The first crack in his composure had appeared —*pry, pry, pry!*

"Yeah, so what?" I said, keeping my eyes fierce, determined. "There's nothing wrong with my cat."

Peter laughed bitterly, then pulled his shirt aside to show the deep claw marks from Octo-Cat's attack last week.

"Fine, okay." I had to fight hard to keep my smirk at bay as I studied the still-red skin. "So, let's start again."

"No," Peter said, turning his chair away from me and pretending to focus on the computer. I could still see him watching me from the corner of his eye, though.

I reached across and shut off his monitor with a humph. "Yes," I insisted.

"If I'd have known you were this much trouble, I never would have—" He stopped abruptly, catching himself before he could get to the climax of that particular sentence.

"Never would have what?" I demanded, leaning even closer. His cloying cologne filled my nostrils, and we were now so close I could have kissed him if I wanted. Not that I'd ever want anything more from Peter than a few answers.

"Forget it," he said, his voice shaking as his face began to turn the same shade of red as the claw marks on his chest.

I poked him again, showing him that I couldn't simply be brushed aside with broken promises and non-answers. "Yeah, you tried to make me forget, didn't you? But I'm not as pliable as you think I am."

"Will you just shut up?" Peter squeaked, his eyes widening in obvious terror. After clearing his throat, he leaned in close and whispered in my ear, "Stop prying into my secrets. Otherwise, I might just have to share yours with all of Blueberry Bay. You got me?"

I nodded slowly, not knowing whether he was bluffing or dead serious but also preferring not to find out. It didn't matter, though, because he did that wavy finger thing under the desk and suddenly I just didn't care anymore.

It wasn't until I got home that evening that I remembered about the digital recorder I'd stashed in my bra. Thank goodness for my tendency to whip that thing off the moment I stepped through the door.

"Did you get some good scoop during your walkabout?" I asked Nan when I got home some hours later.

She rolled her eyes, but smiled. "Nothing yet, but we'll be back out there tomorrow."

Octo-Cat huffed. "Maybe she will, but I'm done. Please tell me you got something out of Peter today." He looked up at me with huge pleading eyes, and I wish I had a better answer for him than *I don't remember.*

"I have this recording," I said, holding up the small item I'd palmed after finding it in my bra.

"Oh, goodie!" Nan cried. "The perfect dinner theater." She tilted her head to the side and let out a chuckle. "Only for lunch."

I laughed, too, and flipped on the recorder, hoping I'd managed to catch something good. Thankfully, it was only a matter of minutes before Peter's and my conversation from earlier that morning played back through the tiny speaker.

Some of the words were drowned out by the rustle of my shirt fabric, but the message still came through loud and clear. Peter knew that I knew something, and he was terrified of me finding out anything more.

"All right," Octo-Cat said following Peter's final whispered threat. "I'm taking the lead on this one."

"Wait. What do you mean?" I sputtered. Octo-Cat had never taken the lead before, and the fact he wanted to now scared me worse than anything I'd seen yet. "What's your plan?"

He sat before me on the table, flexing the claws on one of his front paws and staring at them with delight. "I'm sure you already know that cats are great at everything. And, lucky for you, I'm even greater than most cats. But do you know what I'm greatest at?"

I shook my head, hoping he would just get on with it. Octo-Cat considered himself the greatest genius and talent of our time, so he could literally be talking about anything right about now.

"Stalking my prey," he answered with a sinister smile. "I smell a rat, and you better believe I'm going to make him my dinner."

I continued to stare blankly at Octo-Cat, not sure whether he was done or what he'd even meant by the things he'd said so far.

He sighed and rolled his eyes. "*Peter.* I'm talking about Peter."

"You're going to eat him?" I ground out, trying so hard not to laugh.

"No, it's just..." The tabby groaned. "I was going for a poetic moment there and you kind of ruined it. Can you please get with the program already?"

"Yes, sorry," I murmured, then waited as he went through his entire speech again. When he got to the part about smelling a rat and making it his dinner, I brought a hand to my chest and pretended to swoon.

"My hero," I said overdramatically.

Octo-Cat smiled proudly. "And don't you forget it."

Oh, of all the things I'd forgotten lately, this was one thing I'd never be able to erase from my memory—no matter how much I might want to.

Whatever his plan, I just hoped that my cat—*my hero*—would be safe.

12

That evening Octo-Cat sent me out for a bit of last-minute shopping. He'd requested an Apple Watch, of all things. Now, if you think people can be snobby about their preference for Macs, multiply that by one hundred and you'll have a good sense of how devoted my tabby was to his particular electronics brand of choice.

Sometimes I regretted ever giving him that iPad.

Of course, I had to drive to the next town over to reach the closest big-box electronics store, and I may have gotten laughed at by the employee who'd been assigned to help me.

"You want an Apple Watch for your cat?" he asked incredulously for the third time that conversation. Seemed he thought I was too stupid to understand the question.

I decided to offer a bit more of an explanation to help get us past the whole laughing and customer-shaming episode. "Yeah, I need to attach it to his collar so I can track where he goes when he's outside."

"And it has to be Apple?" he asked, gasping for air between laughs. "There are way cheaper options that are made specifically for pets."

My brow pinched in frustration. Clearly, this man had never been owned by a cat. *The poor oaf.*

"My cat really prefers Apple products whenever possible," I answered quietly, hoping that we wouldn't attract any other clueless employees before my purchase was made. "Can we please just hurry?"

"Yeah, sure. There's a slight problem, though." He stopped laughing and offered me a piteous expression. "The current generation of Apple Watches have to be tethered to a phone in order to work long range."

"Meaning?"

"Meaning it won't work for what you want," he explained somewhat impatiently.

I glanced around the emptying store. Soon

closing time would be upon us, which meant I needed to make a relatively quick decision. I could cater to my cat's ego—or to his safety. You may think the correct choice would have been obvious, but it was a harder decision than you could possibly imagine.

"Okay, show me the pet GPS units," I decided aloud.

The worker smirked as he led me over to a glass case at the end of the aisle where we'd been standing this whole time. I chose the one that looked most like it could be an Apple product and pointed to where it sat inside the display case.

"Ooh. Great choice," the worker said with a nod of affirmation. "It's our best reviewed model."

"Yeah, that's great," I said dismissively before lowering my voice and saying, "I'll slip you a twenty if you can help me with something."

He put both hands up and took a giant step back. "I hope you're not trying to bribe me so that I'll steal from my store." He lowered his voice, came back beside me, and leaned in close. "Not saying I won't do it. Just that the price has to be right."

"What? No." I searched around for the security cameras, which were of course trained right on us. "I already told you, my cat is really committed to

Apple products. So, do you maybe have a leftover sticker or something we can use to cover up the real logo and replace it with Apple's?"

His eyes widened with surprise. Yup, he'd definitely never been owned by a cat. "Um, maybe," he mumbled as he glanced around for an escape route.

"Listen, I know I sound crazy. I promise I'm not." I smiled, hoping he'd see just how harmless I really was. "Not that it even really matters," I continued quickly. "Can you please just help me make this look like an Apple product?"

After a little more back and forth—and ultimately raising the bribe to forty dollars—the worker agreed to help. By the time I was done, I had a passable new accessory for Octo-Cat that I decided I'd tell him was the new Apple Pet. I stashed the instruction manual in my glove compartment and tossed the box in the trashcan outside. I'd just tell him it was the floor model, that we'd gotten the very last one.

He'd like that, the whole exclusivity of his new toy.

Sure enough, my cat was overjoyed when I presented him with his new collar charm that evening. "The Apple Pet. Wow," he cooed. "It's even more beautiful than I ever could have imagined."

"And you're one of the very first to get one," I added, ignoring the fact that he'd probably be the only cat ever with this particular Frankenstein of a GPS tracker.

Nan helped us test it out by watching the tracker on her phone while I drove Octo-Cat around for a few minutes. When we returned she showed me the exact path we'd driven mapped out on her phone. It looked like everything was in place for his big solo mission.

"Be safe," I said the next morning, unable to resist the urge to give him a big hug and a kiss between his ears.

"Angela, really," he ground out while wriggling free of my arms. "The Apple Pet offers the latest state-of-the-art technology. Combine that with my superior intellect, agility, and stamina, and we'll have this case solved by sundown."

I almost felt bad lying to him but knew he'd do better thinking he had Apple on his side. The plan was for him to drive with me to work that morning and then hang around outside the office, hidden among some bushes. Later, he'd slip into Peter's car when he came out at the end of his shift and secretly accompany him to wherever he decided to go that evening.

I personally hoped it would be the lair.

Nan and I both had the app on our phones so that we could follow Octo-Cat's location, and I'd also told him that I would pick him up at midnight, no matter where he was or what was happening at the time. I refused to leave him unassisted for the entire night, especially since Peter appeared more than a little bit unstable judging by all the interactions I'd had with him so far.

"Are you sure?" I asked him one more time as we pulled into the tiny parking lot outside the firm.

The determination in Octo-Cat's gaze didn't waver. "Of course I'm sure. You need me."

"Yes," I repeated. "I need you. So, please be careful and make sure you come home safe."

"Angela, I..." His voice cracked and he bowed his head, then he dragged his sandpaper tongue along my hand in a quick show of affection that practically melted my heart.

"Nothing of this later," he whispered while waiting for me to open the door and set him loose.

I was too stunned to say anything more as I watched him trot away and take cover in the greenery around my office.

After a deep, calming breath, I headed into the office and fought back my urge to start checking the app right away. Nan had eyes on him, too. He would be okay.

Of course, Peter came into work late for the first time since I'd known him. Those forty-odd minutes of thinking our plan would have to wait another day just about killed me, too. When Peter finally did show up for work, he studiously ignored me, even going so far as to pop some earbuds in as an excuse not to talk to me.

Well, that suited me just fine.

I waited as patiently as I could for my half-shift to end, then raced home and sat with Nan as we both watched the unblinking dot that represented Octo-Cat's location on our phones.

"Oh, it's moving!" Nan shouted later that afternoon while we were both enjoying a cup of hot tea with homemade cookies to top off the light snack. Sure enough, the little dot had left the office and was now crawling down Main Street.

I glanced at the time displayed on the top of my phone screen. "But it's too early," I protested. "Peter is supposed to work until five."

"Not today, it seems," Nan said with a half-hearted shrug. Her eyes, however, shone with excitement as she watched the little dot continue its journey.

In fact, we both fell silent as we tracked the dot along the screen. It turned down a series of side roads before finally coming to a stop.

"Zoom in," I told Nan. "What address is that?"

She clicked the dot, and the app gave us the exact street and house number.

"That must be where he lives," I said, taking a quick picture of the screen in case we needed this information for later. "Good to know for future."

"What if he just does a Netflix and chill?" Nan asked, worry lining her aged forehead.

"Who told you about Netflix and chill?" I asked in horror.

Nan waved a hand dismissively. "One of the guys at Bingo. He said it's what all the kids are doing these days. I'm glad you'd rather read than rot your brain with all that TV."

I nodded and hid a smile behind my hand. It was best that Nan stayed innocent as long as I could keep her that way.

Unfortunately, it looked like she was right—at least when it came to what she assumed she'd meant earlier. The dot remained idle for hours. Poor Octo-Cat must have been going out of his mind just sitting there and waiting for Peter to do something skeezy.

I yawned more than once, wondering if Nan and I would have to take shifts to watch the unmoving dot until it was finally time to go and retrieve Octo-Cat at midnight.

How unthrilling and—even worse—unhelpful.

I had all but declared today's mission a bust, when suddenly the dot began to move again.

13

"They're headed downtown!" I shouted, recognizing the path after the dot took a few sharp turns and swung back onto Main Street. I grabbed my phone and rushed toward the door, not even taking the time to slip my feet into my tennis shoes properly.

"I'm coming, too, dear," Nan insisted in that sugar-sweet way of hers as she floated over.

"No way," I insisted right back, albeit with far more hostility. "We need you at home base in case there's any trouble. Keep watching that dot!" I called over my shoulder as I slammed the door shut behind me and made a beeline straight to my car.

If Peter and Octo-Cat were headed toward the lair, then I wanted to be there, too. I kept my phone hooked in its holster and watched the GPS app the entire time I drove. Luckily, Peter made a pit stop, which meant I miraculously managed to beat him downtown. I parked around the corner and then hid myself beside the dumpster in that same alley I now knew led to the magical lair.

I watched breathlessly as the blinking dot approached my location.

Closer, closer...

They should have been right upon me now, but I could see neither Peter nor Octo-Cat. Instead, a humongous pit bull burst into the alley and charged straight toward me. I was so shocked by his sudden arrival that it took me a second to realize his sharp and shiny teeth held something clenched between them.

My cat!

Oh my gosh, this abnormally large dog was carrying Octo-Cat by the scruff of his neck, and he looked mad. Tough, too.

"Please, Mr. Dog," I said, my voice squeaking even though I wanted to appear as strong as possible in that moment. "Please don't hurt us."

The dog locked eyes with me and growled a warning.

I froze in place the way the Girl Scouts had

trained me to do in case of a wild animal attack. Would this dog bite me? Kill me? And why was he still clinging so tight to my cat?

The door to the lair opened and the menacing dog hurled Octo-Cat down the stairway. A sickening crack followed as Octo-Cat hit the ground below. *No!*

"Get in there. Now!" someone growled at me. The voice sounded like Peter's, but it had to belong to someone else, right? Maybe Moss stood nearby just out of sight.

I still couldn't move, although now I was more afraid for Octo-Cat than for myself. Was he okay after that savage fall? What did the dog want with him? And how did it know about the lair?

"Angela!" Octo-Cat cried from the distance. "Angela, don't! It's a trap!"

Oh, Octo-Cat! He was okay. I wanted to cry for joy, but I still couldn't move.

"I said get in there!" the voice came again, and then the pit bull head-butted me down the staircase. The door slammed shut and disappeared. Even if I finally got my wits about me, I couldn't have escaped if I wanted to.

The pit bull stood seething with rage at the top of the stairs. "I knew you would be trouble," he said. This time I knew for sure the voice had come from the dog. It was speaking to me, much in the same way Octo-Cat did. But how? How was I understanding him? And why did he sound so much like Peter?

Octo-Cat lay across the room just a few feet from the far wall. He struggled to stand but fell back on his side with a gasp of pain.

"Thought cats were always supposed to land on their feet?" the dog taunted us in Peter's voice once again.

"That's a low blow and you know it," Moss said, appearing suddenly from the shadows. "What's got your fur in a twist?"

"Caught one of yours creeping about my territory," the pit bull answered with a nod toward Octo-Cat. "Figured I'd bring him here and let you deal with him, seeing as he's one of your kind."

Moss tensed, then narrowed his eyes and stared the dog down. "I'm not doing it this way. Show yourself."

I whipped my face back toward the dog, but not fast enough to see whatever transformation had occurred. Now it was Peter who stood crouched on all fours exactly where the dog had been. My eyes bulged and strained, trying desperately to find a way to explain what they'd just seen.

"Take a picture," Peter said with a wry smile. "It will last longer."

A picture? That wasn't actually a bad idea. I still had my phone clenched in my hand from tracking the GPS app, so I raised it toward Peter and—

He slapped it right out of my hand. "Seriously? Ever hear of sarcasm?" he demanded, curling his lip in disgust.

"Okay, enough!" Moss cried, yanking me away from Peter with surprising strength and lifting me up high so I dangled right in front of his face. "*You.* I've met you before. Didn't you say Peter was the one who invited you here in the first place?"

I nodded slowly, not breaking eye contact. Although I was still terrified, I knew I stood a better chance of eliciting sympathy from Moss than from Peter. Could I somehow convince him to let us go without further harm? I had to try.

"Yes, yes!" I shouted. "He told me to come here last weekend, but then he didn't show up!"

Moss sucked air in through his teeth. "That's bad form, dog. Really bad form." Turning back to me, he said, "I thought you were one of us. Why are you hanging out with *him?*"

"One of..."

"He's a cat," Octo-Cat informed me with a wheeze. "I thought I smelled it on him the first time we met, but I didn't know that people could, could..."

"Become animals?" Peter asked, changing into a dog again so quick I still couldn't tell how it was done. He rounded on Octo-Cat and raised his hackles. "Not so tough now are you, big shot?"

"Hey!" I cried, straining to break free so I could defend my poor, injured kitty. "Leave him alone!"

Moss groaned and set me back on my feet. "You know the lair is neutral territory," he said to Peter. "So knock it off already."

When I glanced back toward Moss, he'd transformed into a stunning long-haired cat with those same ethereal green eyes.

"Can you two please stop doing that?" Octo-Cat whimpered from his place on the floor. "It's making me dizzy."

"Are you okay?" I hurried over to him, then knelt down to lift him into my arms.

Octo-Cat allowed me to cradle him to my chest, which he'd never done before.

"I'm fine," he croaked. "Just down a life is all."

Seeing the intense worry that, no doubt, filled

my expression, he let out a dry chuckle. “Hey, don’t look so worried. I still have almost half of them left. Just give me another few seconds here and I’ll be back to fighting form.”

“No,” I whispered, pressing my forehead to his and fighting against the hot tears that threatened to spill. “No more fights. This stops now.”

“Or what?” Peter asked with a sneer as he observed Octo-Cat’s and my tender moment with thinly veiled hatred.

“I said knock it off already!” When Moss hissed, it sounded like air being let out of old tires. “We agreed to work together when it came to Glendale.”

“Then she’s a threat to us both,” Peter spat, human again and with his arms crossed tightly against his chest.

Moss studied me with a frown. “Well, what do you want me to do about it? Lock her up and let the council decide?”

Peter gave one emphatic nod. “Yes, that’s exactly what I want you to do.”

“Fine,” Moss said, returning to his human form faster than a snap. He picked me up and pushed me into the corner of the room. I tried to charge after him but was stuck behind some kind of invisible barrier.

"How do you like the fishbowl?" Peter asked with an evil smile I wanted to slap right off his cruel face. If I hadn't liked him before, now I outright hated him. I would never be able to forgive him for hurting my best fur friend.

"We still don't know who sent her or why, so maybe we should stop antagonizing her until we get some answers," Moss pointed out, though he sounded unsure of the words even as he spoke them.

"What's going on?" I cried, still clutching Octo-Cat tightly to my chest. My tears had broken free now and drove down my cheeks in hot trails.

Moss bit his lip, then turned to Peter. "We at least need to remove the glamor if we're going to hold her here. Too long without it and she'll go crazy. You know that, Peter."

"Fine." Peter snapped his fingers and that old, dank basement suddenly transformed into a posh underground club. Finally, I could see why they called it the lair. Cherry wood paneling lined the walls and the floor had been laid with marble. Sure enough, Octo-Cat and I were in a fishbowl just as Peter had described. The tiny room that imprisoned us was made of glass on two sides and hard wall on the others.

I jumped back to my feet and pounded on the thick glass. “Let us out!” I screamed.

“Not a chance,” Peter said with a sinister laugh. He was definitely enjoying this way too much. Had this been his plan all along? But why go to such lengths to steal my crummy paralegal job?

“We can’t let you go just yet. Not until the council decides,” Moss said with an apologetic shrug.

Again with the council? Who were they? And what would they decide?

I looked past Moss in a frantic search for some kind of escape route. That was when I realized we had an audience.

14

The lair appeared to be a boy's club. I didn't spot a single woman among the spectators, although I supposed any of the many cats or dogs could have been female. I sank down in the corner where the two wood walls joined together and tried not to look intimidated by the night's bizarre turn of events.

After nursing his wounds a bit longer, Octo-Cat slipped out of my arms and began to pace the length of the glass. "Chin up. Don't let them see you break," he instructed, almost as if he'd been imprisoned before. I'd definitely be asking about his kittenhood once we were free of this whole mess.

"What happened when you were with Peter?" I

asked quietly, hoping nobody else would be able to pick up on our whispered conversation.

"Oh, Angela. It was all my fault." He turned to me suddenly, immense sorrow reflecting in his normally steady amber gaze. "Everything would have been fine, but on the drive downtown, Peter took a turn really fast and I couldn't help it. I-I-I-I yowled!"

My cat now blubbered in earnest as if realizing for the first time ever that he wasn't actually perfect. *The poor thing.* This entire experience had to be as life-altering for him as it was proving to be for me, perhaps even more.

Octo-Cat tried to keep a stiff upper lip as he continued, but broke down at several points in his story. "He slammed on the brakes and dragged me out by-by-by my scruff, then threw me in the trunk for the rest of the drive. I m-m-made a plan to leap at him and go for the eyes when we stopped, but it wasn't hi-hi-him that opened the trunk. It was the other him."

The dog. I still couldn't believe Peter could change into that pit bull at will. This was the stuff of fairytales, and honestly, it didn't belong in my picture-perfect little coastal town.

"Did you learn anything good?" I asked as I

watched my cat continue to pace back and forth. I hated how worked up he was, but also found myself quite relieved that he was moving and talking like normal again.

"Not until we got here," Octo-Cat answered with a sigh. "But I'm afraid I was so out of sorts after I c-c-crashed down the stairs that I missed most of it. And..." He sniffed hard, then tried again. "And!"

He broke down into incomprehensible sobs once again. His shoulders heaved with distress as he struggled—and failed—to get the words out.

"It's okay," I cooed, tapping my fingers softly on the ground to call him to me. "You can tell me anything. It's not going to make me love you any less."

Octo-Cat trotted up to my side, then turned his face away and mumbled. "My new Apple Pet took a lot of the impact and it-it-it... it shattered, Angela!" he finished at last.

"Oh, Octavius," I said, using his full first name to help remind him of who he was. I hated seeing him so broken up like this. "Please don't worry about that. In fact, if it makes you feel better, that wasn't an Apple at all."

He turned back toward me, his eyes wide now

for a different reason—complete and unadulterated horror. "*What?*" he demanded.

Oh, no. I was in such a rush to help him that I hadn't thought about how this particular revelation would impact me. I should have just kept my big mouth shut. I guessed now that the cat was out of the bag, though...

"It wasn't Apple," I said again, trapped by the intense scrutiny of his angry gaze. Now I was the one who had a stutter. "Apple Watches n-n-need to be tethered to a phone to work out of range, and I w-wanted you to be safe, so—"

"Angela!" he shouted, then evened his voice out and went into full-fledged lecture mode. I hated lecture mode. It meant that he was too angry to even insult me now. "If you'd gotten me an Apple like I requested, none of this would have happened in the first place."

"That's not fair," I shot back. The way he'd described being discovered by Peter had absolutely nothing to do with any failings of the GPS.

He pressed his ears back flat against his head and stooped toward the ground. "I can't believe you let me think that *I* could have been the one to mess things up so royally. How could you let me doubt myself like that?"

I hung my head, properly chastised. "I'm s-sorry."

"Sorry isn't good enough, Angela," he said with a small tutting noise. "If you would've followed my very simple, very clear instructions, we wouldn't be in this mess."

At least as I felt worse, he appeared to feel better and better. Perhaps we'd even each other out. "Fine, it's all my fault. Happy?"

Octo-Cat shook his head again, slowly this time. "I thought I'd trained you better."

"You can catch up on my training later," I promised with a giant, unhappy sigh. "Right now we need to focus on finding a way out of here."

"Well, that's easy," he said with a quick shrug.

I scrambled to my feet. "Great! Then tell me."

Octo-Cat deadpanned as he revealed, "There isn't one."

"Great." I let myself sink back to the floor before realizing that maybe I shouldn't just take his word at face value here. "What makes you so sure there's no way out?"

"Magic," he answered matter-of-factly.

"I thought you said you couldn't see magic."

"I can't, but I think maybe now I can feel it a bit." He flexed a paw demonstratively. "Can't you?"

"Well, I..." I closed my eyes and focused on my breathing, trying to see if I felt any different than I had before we'd entered the lair. I gave it a good try, but ultimately came up short. "Yeah... no," I said pathetically, wondering if my cat's newfound ability might be all in his head anyway.

Octo-Cat growled and flicked his tail. "Even so, we just saw one human turn into a dog and another into a cat. We saw this place appear out of nowhere and then get an insta-makeover from dirty dungeon to swanky night club. I think it's safe to say we're in magical territory now."

He had a definite point.

"But what do they want with us?" I mumbled, watching Peter as he laughed and joked with a small group of people I'd never seen before.

"I don't know." Octo-Cat was back to pacing while Peter paused and looked toward me, victory dancing across his face.

I refused to let him win, especially since I didn't fully understand the stakes. "How did Peter even find out about me in the first place?"

"I also don't know that."

I swallowed hard, then asked the toughest question of all. "Are they going to kill us?"

Octo-Cat paused and looked at me over his

shoulder. “Well, they already killed me once, although I don’t think that was intentional.”

“Did you really die back there?”

He nodded grimly. “It was my fifth time.”

“How did you die the other four times?” I asked, having always wondered about this. If we couldn’t break out of our magical prison, then at least we could pass the time learning more about each other’s pasts. It seemed we were always so caught up in our current adventures that we rarely had time to stroll down memory lane side-by-side.

Octo-Cat plopped down, facing me, and I could tell I was in for a good story that would hopefully take my mind off our current predicament. “Well, the first time was at the beach. I—”

One of the glass panels slid to the side with a swish, cutting off what I was sure would be a riveting tale. Perhaps Octo-Cat would be willing to tell it to me later.

The cat version of Moss slipped through the opening, and the moment he’d crossed the barrier, the glass wall slammed shut again.

“What’s going on?” I pleaded, remaining seated so that I was closer to eye level with both cats. “Are you here to help us?”

Moss sat by the glass, leaving a large distance between us. "I can't say for sure, but maybe."

"Maybe what? Maybe you'll help us?" I crawled over to him on my hands and knees, and laughter rose from outside the fishbowl. I didn't care about our audience, though. I only cared about getting help, and Moss still seemed our best chance at that happening.

"Yes," he answered, looking down his nose at me as I scrambled closer. "But first, I have some questions."

"He's going to interrogate us," Octo-Cat translated, even though I didn't need the help. "Just like in the order part of *Law & Order.*"

Moss smiled, and that small gesture put me at ease. He really was a very pretty cat—not that I'd ever admit that aloud near Octo-Cat.

"Yeah, well, things work a little different when it comes to the council," he said, still smiling although something in his expression had changed.

"Different how?" I asked, raising an eyebrow. Slowly, the fear was returning. What did they have planned for us? And how could we get them to change their minds? I no longer much cared about decoding my abilities. These were the new questions I desperately needed answers to.

Moss chuckled, his green eyes boring into mine.

I paused in my tracks and waited for the big reveal.

Finally, Moss stopped laughing and informed us, “For starters, we’re not the good guys.”

I gulped hard, but nothing I did made me feel any better.

We’d been captured, and by a shape-shifting magical gang that seemed to show little regard for the rules.

If we died down here, would anyone ever even know?

I was suddenly so thankful that Octo-Cat’s tracker had broken. At least I knew now that Nan would be safe.

Even if we weren’t.

15

"Who do you work for?" Moss demanded, turning back toward me sharply.

A cheer rose up from the club. I blinked in horror as I noticed close to a dozen people and animals crowd in toward the glass, each vying for the best spot. *Oh, great.* Octo-Cat and I had become the unwitting stars of some kind of twisted, magical reality TV program.

"We ain't telling you nothing!" Octo-Cat shouted, then spat dramatically on the ground. This antic earned him a few polite chuckles from the audience.

"Actually, there's nothing to tell, seeing as we don't work for anyone," I explained, quietly willing

Octo-Cat to ignore the lure of this momentary fame and let me handle things. "Unless Longfellow, Peters, and Associates counts," I added with a forced calm.

"Peters," Moss said, rubbing his chin with a paw. "Interesting."

"Not *that* Peters," I corrected with a quick glance toward the audience. Peter stood just on the other side of the glass, watching with a disturbing hunger in his eyes. "Bethany Peters. She's nice."

"They're all the same, sweetheart," Moss said with a chuckle. Did he know Bethany? Was Bethany—*gasp*—like him? How could that even be possible?

And why did it feel like everyone else was playing out some kind of old-timey movie? Even Octo-Cat had stars in his eyes now that he realized we had an audience.

Me? I just wanted to get home safe and put this whole ordeal behind me. If it meant never learning the truth about my abilities, then so be it. I'd rather be alive than informed.

"Are you really working with the dogs?" Octo-Cat asked, then spit on the ground again. When nobody laughed this time, his expression fell.

"Will you just stop spitting?" I demanded with

an exacerbated sigh. Now I was equal parts annoyed and terrified. I'd much preferred being tied up or held at gunpoint as I had in my previous misadventures. At least then I'd known what I was up against. Here, everyone was crazy and unpredictable, super-powered and spry.

I definitely didn't like my odds, being that I appeared to be the only semi-sane, semi-normal person around.

"You can talk to him," Moss pointed out, narrowing his eyes at me as he tilted his head sideways toward Octo-Cat. We were getting nowhere fast, seeing as Moss wanted to revisit all the previously established facts.

"Yes, but you already knew that," I said, raking my hands through my hair in frustration. "Also, why does it even matter? Obviously, everyone here can talk to him, too."

"Who sent you?" Moss demanded yet again.

I glowered at him as I explained, "You've already asked that, and I've already explained that nobody sent me. Well, except Peter."

"Are you a double agent?"

A low *ooh* swept through the crowd. Apparently, this was a very important question. Too bad I didn't have the slightest idea how to answer it.

"What? I really have no idea what you're talking about."

"Shift," Moss demanded, looking from me to Octo-Cat and back again.

"Um, we can't." I rolled my eyes to show him how ridiculous I found this whole thing.

Octo-Cat spit on the ground again and said, "No can do, fuzz."

Oh, jeez. I had really thought he'd remain silent after his last joke was met with zero applause. I already knew the more he spoke, the longer this would take. Luckily, Moss seemed more interested in me than in my cat.

"Shift," Moss said again, raising a threatening paw with claws fully extended.

I didn't even flinch. "I told you I can't," I said through gritted teeth.

Moss apparently did not like this answer, because he hurled himself at my face and sunk his claws into my cheek.

Peter's voice rose above the others as pain exploded on my cheek. "How do you like it now that the tables are turned?"

Blood dribbled down onto my shirt, but I was too scared to focus on the pain. "You can torture me all you want, but I don't have a different answer to give you," I said through gritted teeth.

"Nobody attacks my human and lives to tell the tale," Octo-Cat shouted, surging forward to tackle Moss.

"Stop!" I screamed at them both. Octo-Cat couldn't take a beating so soon after losing that last life. As noble as I found his choice to defend me, this was one fight I knew he'd lose.

"Just stop!" I begged Moss whose teeth were now at Octo-Cat's throat. "I'll tell you everything I know. It's not much, but I'll tell you."

Octo-Cat backed away, hackles fully raised, his tail so poofy he looked more like a long-haired breed than his usual tabby self.

"Excellent." Moss dragged his claws across the cold marble floor as if to remind me he could still do considerable damage, should we step out of line again. "Now, which one of you is magical?"

"Neither," I answered, throwing my hands over my face defensively. "I never even knew magic existed until this week, and I couldn't even talk to him until about six months ago."

Moss came closer and stood on his hind legs. He pressed his front paws against my chest and peered into my face as he asked, "What happened six months ago?"

"I got zapped by a coffee maker," I answered breathlessly. My cheek had begun to throb from his earlier attack. More than mad, it made me scared.

"And when she woke up, we could understand each other," Octo-Cat finished for me.

"That's rather anti-climactic," Moss said. His voice now had the slightest hint of a twang. If he'd had an accent before, he'd done a wonderful job hiding it. I wondered if the fact it was coming out meant he was every bit as flustered as I felt.

Perhaps Octo-Cat and I could still win this yet.

"But you can't shift?" he asked for what felt like the millionth time in the span of just a few minutes.

I shook my head so hard it hurt. How could I make him—and the others who were still watching hungrily—believe me once and for all? *"No,"* I said with as much emphasis as I could assign to the short, little word. "And I can't do that memory thingy, either."

"The memory... Oh." Moss laughed a full-belly laugh, and the room joined in. "So, you're a normie?" he asked at last, wiping tears away as he fought off the final throws of laughter. Octo-Cat had never been able to produce tears on demand. I wondered if Moss could because he was really a human.

"If that means a normal, ordinary person, then yes," I told him with a stony gaze.

Moss nodded toward Octo-Cat. "And him?"

I nodded again. "Totally normal."

"Excuse you," Octo-Cat hissed, stomping over to join us. "I'm anything but—"

"Shut up!" I shouted at him. This was not the time for that overblown ego of his.

"What are you hiding?" Moss demanded, turning toward Octo-Cat but still watching me from his peripheral vision.

"Nothing. I swear."

He studied Octo-Cat for a moment before breaking out in an unfriendly smile. "Ah, I get it," he concluded. "He's just your average, everyday cat with an unfailingly high opinion of himself."

I let out a breath I hadn't realized I'd been holding in. "Yes. Exactly."

"So, somehow you got hit with magical resonance," he continued.

I couldn't tell whether it was meant to be a question or not. "Sure?"

"And that's why you don't show up on any of

our tracking systems," he continued. "You're a non-magical entity with a single magical ability."

I nodded along. This explanation certainly made sense, seeing as I was sure about only two things here—one, I wasn't magical, and two, I could talk to Octo-Cat.

A collective gasp sounded from the crowd. Why did they find me so interesting, especially when they could all do such extraordinary things themselves?

"Does that happen often?" I asked, suddenly desperate to understand more.

Moss shook his head. "No, it really doesn't. This started six months ago, you say?"

I pumped my head in agreement. Finally, someone would tell me the answers. I could feel them bubbling just beneath the surface. Peter hadn't helped me, but Moss would. I just knew it.

"That's worrying," he said.

"Why?"

"If you were a true magical person, you would have been born that way. If you were hit with some magical residue, it should have faded within twenty-four hours."

"So, what am I then?" I asked as my heart hammered away inside my chest.

"That depends," he said with a thoughtful expression.

"On?" I was so close to begging him for more. Couldn't he see how desperately I needed to know?

"Your cooperation," he answered with a pensive gaze.

Nobody said anything for a few moments until Peter appeared at the edge of the glass. "You're either big trouble," he said with a scowl.

"Or our greatest weapon," Moss finished, his eyes now shining with an evil joy.

"No, no, no. I don't want to be a weapon," I argued, shuffling backward until my back was flat up against the wall.

"What about me?" Octo-Cat asked. "Am I a weapon, too?"

"You?" Moss laughed and shook his head. "You're just an ordinary, everyday tabby cat."

16

Octo-Cat took several steps back until he bumped into the glass. *"No,"* he whispered over and over again. "No, it's not possible."

The crowd roared with laughter but, despite their glee, I could tell my cat was hurting. Badly.

"Don't listen to them," I pleaded, pushing myself to my feet so I could go to him.

He flinched at my touch, then bounded out of reach. "Don't," Octo-Cat said sadly, refusing to look at me.

"Always with the dramatics," Peter said, stalking in on all fours to join us inside the fishbowl. He waved one arm in a circle and the glass turned into a shiny opaque surface, cutting off both the sights and sounds from outside.

"We're alone now," Peter confirmed, sitting down on his haunches. His great tongue lolled from the side of his open maw in clear anticipation.

"It would be easier for me to talk to you if you were human," I said, clenching my eyes shut tight as I turned away. A part of me still didn't want to believe that any of this was happening.

"Have it your way," Peter said coldly.

When I opened my eyes again, both he and Moss had returned to their human forms while Octo-Cat remained turned away and sulking in his corner.

"Now are you going to cooperate or what?" Moss asked, his green eyes taking in my every move.

"Or would you rather do this the hard way?" Peter asked. Apparently, we'd returned to their previous good cop, bad cop routine. But I wouldn't be fooled this time. Moss had already admitted that neither of them was good, and thus it stood to reason that neither of them would help us out of the kindness of their hearts. They wanted something, and I just hoped it wouldn't be too high a price to pay.

I bit down hard on my lip as I watched them watch me. And then I couldn't take the studied silence any longer. A million questions weighed on the tip of my tongue, and I let the first few spill out into the open air. "What do you want from me? And if you're not the good guys, then who are you? Are you going to let us go?"

Peter puckered his lips unattractively and made a condescending tutting noise. "So many questions when you won't even answer our one simple request."

"Cooperate," Octo-Cat murmured from across the room. He had his forehead pressed to the wall as if that was the only way he could remain upright. I'd never seen him like this. Not even close. At this point, I knew I needed to do or say whatever it took to get us out of here, to get him help.

"Fine," I answered, keeping my gaze on that poor forlorn tabby to remind myself why I was suddenly so willing to assist my enemy. "What do you need from me?"

"Money," Peter said with a smirk. "Lots of it."

I faltered at this. After all this hocus pocus nonsense, were they really only after my money? "I-I don't have much at present, but if you'll allow me to make monthly payments, I can—"

"Not from you," Moss amended. "But *rather by way* of you."

That's when all the pieces began clicking into place. Finally, I could see the picture for what it was. "The robberies downtown," I murmured, unsurprised that this gang would stoop so low but somewhat disappointed in myself for not figuring it out sooner.

Peter licked his chops even though he was still in human form. "The first several were easy, but the jewelry store has a magic-sensing alarm."

"That's why you couldn't get in the other night," I said. And that's why we'd seen those dogs running back and forth through town during our stakeout. All of it, everything fit together so neatly, and Moss had just delivered the tidying bow.

"Hey, try not to judge us too harshly," the cat shifter said with wide eyes. "It was invisible, so we didn't know it was there until it was too late."

Oh, I was judging them all right, just not for this reason. "How did you get into the other stores?" I asked, emboldened by the thrill of this new information.

"Glamor," Moss said simply as if this one word answered every question. I thought I recalled reading about glamor in one of the fairy books I'd enjoyed as a kid, but that was back when I hadn't known that magic could be real, that it could also be dangerous.

It explained so much now that I thought about it, though. How the dingy basement had transformed into our current surroundings, how Peter had tampered with my mind on more than one occasion. Was that how they changed into their animal forms as well?

I wanted to know more, but more than that, I just wanted to be free.

"I don't see how I can help," I said, raising my fingers to my mouth and chomping at the nails to offer myself some sort of small comfort.

"Well, that part's easy," Moss said, stretching from side to side. "We have the code for the human alarm, and you're not magic so you won't trigger the magical one."

"Won't they catch me on the security camera, though?" I wondered aloud.

Moss shook his head. "Not if you send in the cat."

"I don't want to steal," I argued. Couldn't they see that I was a good person? That, despite the fact that I may have once absorbed some magical resonance, I was nothing like either of them?

That was when Peter snapped at me, lunging closer. "Do you want to live?"

If Moss hadn't caught his arm and pulled him back, I have no doubt he'd have attacked me.

"Just do it, Angela," Octo-Cat mumbled into the wall. "It's too late for me, but you can still save yourself."

Oh. My heart broke for him all over again. He was right. I needed to stop dawdling. I could still save us both—and I would.

"When?" I asked, licking my lips.

A giant smile slithered across Moss's freckled face. "Tonight."

"And then you'll let us go?" I asked, watching him closely for any sign that he might be lying.

"Yeah, you're really of no use to us beyond this one thing," Moss said with a quick, reassuring nod.

"But if we run into another magical alarm, we just may call on you again," Peter added afterward.

I crossed my arms over my chest and pouted. "I don't want to be at your beck and call."

"Do you want everyone to know your crazy little secret?" Peter asked, cracking his knuckles so that I would look at his strong fists.

I bit my lip to keep from speaking. I had wanted to keep my ability a secret, but now it felt like the lesser of two evils. If the only thing Peter had over me was threatening to tell, then maybe I should just tell everyone myself.

"Fine," I said through clenched teeth as I motioned toward Octo-Cat. "I'll do it, but first he and I need some time alone."

"So you can plan your escape? No way." Peter transformed back into the dog and bared his teeth at me.

Moss put his hand on top of the pit bull's head. "You go. I'll stay and supervise."

Peter continued to growl, and Moss smacked him upside the head. "They may not be magic, but they're still cat people. It's best I handle this. Now get."

Peter whimpered as he shuffled away with his tail tucked between his legs. I would have laughed at the sight if I hadn't still been so scared.

"I don't get it," I said to Moss, once the opaque glass closed again. "If you hate each other so much, then why do you work together?"

He sighed as if he didn't like it much more than I did. "It's part of the truce that the council enacted many years ago."

"Who is this council you keep talking about?"

"The court that governs the magic world," he

answered, unbothered by all my questions now that I'd agreed to help carry out their robbery and Peter had left us on our own.

"The good guys?" I asked hopefully.

Moss nodded. "Yes, the good guys. Bad guys, too, though. In our world, they work together."

I shook my head, unable to understand. "But that doesn't make any sense."

"Maybe not to you, but if the magical world is to survive, we need perfect balance in all we do. The good with the bad. The light with the dark. The fact with the fiction."

"The cat with the dog?" I asked, cracking a smile.

"Indeed," Moss confirmed solemnly.

I thought this over, and it did seem to make sense, even though Moss and Peter's world obviously worked differently from the one I knew. "Could you maybe give us a few moments to talk this out?"

We both watched Octo-Cat who still had his forehead pressed against the cold wood of the wall.

"He needs me," I explained, keeping my eyes trained on my depressed feline companion the entire time. "And he also needs a pep talk if you want him to have any part of this."

Moss situated himself in the other corner of the room, then looked to the side and mumbled over his shoulder, "Go ahead."

I walked over to Octo-Cat and sat down beside him. "Rough day, huh?"

He let out one sarcastic laugh, then quickly fell silent again.

"They don't know you, Octavius. Not like I do." I begged him to understand, to not let them break him. He'd been through so much before—too much for this to be the thing that finally brought him down.

"They said I'm ordinary," he choked out.

"They're wrong," I said firmly, stroking my hand across his fur.

"They can do such amazing things, things I never even dreamt of before," he explained, still unwilling to meet my eyes.

"But you can do pretty amazing things yourself. And without any magic to push you over the top."

Finally, he turned toward me so that his cheek rested against the wall. "Are you saying their magic is a cheat?"

"Yes," I said with a huge smile. I loved when he helped to fill in the blanks for me. I could convince Octo-Cat of anything just so long as I appealed to his special brand of cat logic. I bobbed my head in continued agreement. *"Definitely."*

He sniffed and cautioned a glance toward Moss. "If they're cheating, then they have to be disqualified."

"You're right," I said. I wasn't sure what game we were talking about but figured it must be the competition for best cat in the room or something. "They should totally be disqualified."

At last, a small smile played across his lips. "And if they're disqualified, then I'm the winner by default."

"The best cat in the entire world!" I said without missing a beat.

He stood and pushed himself away from the wall. "Okay, Angela. I'm on board."

We locked eyes and smiled at each other—partners, friends, and now co-criminals, it seemed. "Let's do this," we said in unison.

17

We were held in the fishbowl for a couple more hours while everyone waited for peak criminal hours to approach. Nan must have been going crazy with worry. I could only hope we'd be back to her soon.

First, we just had to commit one teensy, little burglary, then Octo-Cat and I would be home free. Once Octo-Cat was feeling like himself again and ready to help, Peter walked us through what he expected of us, step by excruciating step.

Apparently, this plan had been in the works for quite some time. It made me wonder if Peter would have abducted us, had we not followed him downtown to begin with.

The burglary would go down like this...

I'd enter through the back door with the key they'd filched and had copied earlier that week. Next, I'd deactivate the alarm with the code they'd give me, then open the door for Octo-Cat who would slip in and begin knocking all the jewelry from the cases out onto the floor.

When he gave his signal, I would rush in wearing a crazy green bodysuit that covered everything, including my face, and Octo-Cat would stand guard while I shoved our bounty into the oversized purse the good folks at the lair had provided me with.

Once I returned to the street, one of them would use their glamor to hide me from view—apparently that was easier to do with me already wearing a walking green screen get-up—and we'd all run back toward our underground hiding spot. As soon as Moss and Peter confirmed that I'd completed the job to their satisfaction, they'd wipe our memories and release us back to our ordinary, everyday lives.

This, of course, was provided that everything went perfectly.

And also that Peter wouldn't trick me into helping him again in the future. And, well, I trusted him just about as far as I could throw him.

Oh, how I hated everything about this night.

Mr. Gable, the old man who owned the jewelry store, had always been kind to me whenever I'd passed him on the street. He'd even helped to pick out the heart-shaped locket my parents had purchased as a gift for my eighteenth birthday. Whether or not he had the right kind of insurance to deal with getting robbed blind, he still didn't deserve for this to happen.

No one did.

Now, obviously, Mr. Gable had to be magical, too. Otherwise he wouldn't have known to add a magic-seeking alarm to his store's security system. And that made me wonder... could he transform into an animal, too? Use glamor to hide both thoughts and things?

The old shopkeeper had been a part of this town for as long as I could remember, and it unnerved me to think that magic had always been so close by without me ever even suspecting it. So, was he one of the good guys or the bad guys? And did it even matter which side he ascribed to if the two opposing teams always worked together anyway?

I felt so lost in this strange, new world.

I really just wanted to get back to my normal life as soon as possible.

By the time, Moss returned to let us out of the

fishbowl, I was ready to do whatever they said if it meant freeing ourselves faster. Octo-Cat was in a better mood now and actually seemed a bit excited about the mission that we'd been forced into carrying out.

"I've always suspected they call it cat burglary for a reason," he quipped as Moss joined up with Peter, and together they escorted us toward the jewelry shop.

I wanted to run but knew it would be useless. We didn't have a level playing field here, and the only way I could emerge safely from this situation was to do exactly as I had been told.

"Are you ready?" Moss asked, tightening his hold on my arm as we peered around the corner. "You understand the plan?"

Peter gripped my other arm just as tightly. I would definitely have bruises the next morning, provided it ever came. "If you try any funny stuff, we'll know. And I promise that I will personally make your life a living hell after that."

I nodded glumly. "Understood." I did not doubt the sincerity of that particular statement. Peter had been gunning for me ever since that first awkward morning in the office. Probably even before then, too.

"The cat stays with us until you've deactivated the normie alarm," Moss said. "Got it?"

Octo-Cat struggled underneath Moss's arm but had no words of encouragement to offer me as I readied myself for action.

"Yes, I've got it," I said with an angry stare.

Finally, both Moss and Peter let me go and shoved me down the alley.

The little metal key burned in my palm, the only witness to my sad fall from grace. These people had hurt me and my cat. They'd hurt others, and still they weren't finished. They'd probably never be finished.

Was it really worth continuing that chain of destruction and greed?

And what if I did everything they said, but they kept us prisoner, anyway?

Anything was possible, I supposed. Nothing was guaranteed in life, especially when working hand-in-hand with such unsavory characters. Still, I had to at least try to get myself home in one piece. After all, it wasn't just me they held captive. Octo-Cat was firmly in their clutches as well, and he definitely wouldn't be able to take four more lifetimes of being told he was nothing special.

I'd reached the door now. This was really

happening, and it was happening now. The key slipped seamlessly into the lock, and I sucked in a deep breath as I twisted the knob open. Inside the doorway, the alarm sounded with a warning chirp. I had ten seconds to punch in the correct code, just as Peter had instructed.

I closed my eyes and saw the numbers appear before me. Feeling my way around the pad, I found the first number and pressed it inward.

With another deep breath, I punched the second digit. I opened my eyes again. I could do this. I was doing this. Doing something bad didn't make me a bad person, not when I'd been threatened and tricked into helping commit this crime.

I was halfway through my first task. Just two more buttons and only a handful of seconds left.

By the time I pressed the third button, my hairline had moistened with sweat. My breathing slowed not because I was calm, but because every single inhalation became more and more difficult to take. My head spun and vision blurred as I regarded the keypad before me.

Only one more digit, then this—or at least *this part*—would be over.

I raised my index finger, trying not to focus on

the way it shook as I moved it toward the array of buttons.

I closed my eyes and pressed it down hard...

On the panic button.

An ear-piercing siren sounded overhead, but I made no effort to get away. *Let them find me here.*

A voice sounded over the speakers, but I was too clammed up to say anything. I only hoped that Moss and Peter hadn't punished Octo-Cat for my insubordination, that he still believed in himself enough to fight back.

It only took minutes for a battle-ready Officer Bouchard to arrive on the scene. When he saw me waiting with my hands held in the sky, he took a step back in surprise. "Angie. What are you doing here? Did you see who broke in?"

I nodded stoically. "Yes, me."

"You?" He stopped to scratch his head and wrinkled his nose. "That's not possible."

"I willfully entered with this key." I tossed the illegal copy his way.

He pulled it closer with his foot but didn't bend down to pick it up. "Then why did you hit the panic alarm?"

"I didn't have a choice," I sobbed. "They threatened me and my cat."

"I figured it was something like that," Officer Bouchard said, worry lining his brow. "Put your hands down. I'm not going to arrest you."

I took a deep breath and let my hands fall to my sides. Tears had snuck up on me again. But I didn't care about me. More than anything, I was desperately worried about Octo-Cat. Had I just signed his death warrant by refusing to play along with the magicfolks' devious scheme?

"Who made you do this, Angie?" the officer asked kindly.

I took a deep breath. This was it. Peter had promised to make my life hell. What he didn't know is that stooping to his insidious level would have done the exact same thing. I'd never be able to live with myself knowing I'd done something so wrong. Whether or not he wiped my memory clear, my heart would always know that something was wrong.

This was the time to make sure that the bad guys went down for their crimes. Even if Officer Bouchard didn't understand the full extent of how they'd carried out the burglaries downtown, I hoped my testimony would be enough to get them arrested—and punished.

"Peter Peters and Moss…I don't know his last name," I told him, my voice clear and sure as a bell.

"It's okay, Angie," he said, placing a comforting hand on my shoulder. "You're safe now."

Maybe I was, but I still had no idea what had happened to my poor cat.

18

Officer Bouchard gave me a ride home in his cruiser, seeing as my captors had relieved me of both my phone and my car keys. When we pulled up, Nan raced down the porch steps and pulled me to her chest.

"I was so worried," she sobbed into my hair, then reared back and hit me on the chest. *"Never, ever* do that to me again."

"Thank you, Officer," I said with a small yet appreciative smile, even though inside my heart was still broken. Every minute that ticked away without me knowing the location of my best feline friend only broke it further. It had been nearly an hour since Officer Bouchard found me with my hands up inside of Mr. Gable's shop. After I'd given him Peter's name, he let me search the downtown area far and wide while he called in the new lead.

Sadly, despite my frantic searching, Octo-Cat was still nowhere to be found.

"Where's Octavius?" Nan asked, leading me inside with one arm draped across my shoulders.

"I-I-I don't know," I sputtered.

"Oh, dear," she said, her mouth pressed in a thin line. "First tea, then you can catch me up on everything."

I waited on the couch while Nan tended to the kettle. A short while later, she pressed a mug of hibiscus tea into my waiting hands.

"For strength," she said, settling in beside me on the stiff couch. "Now go ahead whenever you're ready, dear."

I'd held back in sharing the full details of my story with Officer Bouchard, but with Nan, I spared no detail. By the time I reached the part where I'd decided to inform the authorities rather than give in to Peter and Moss's demands, Nan wore a giant grin.

"I'm so proud of you, dear one. You did everything right." She hugged me to her side and pressed a kiss onto my forehead.

"But Octo-Cat," I argued, feeling like the worst pet owner in the entire world.

Nan waited for me to look up at her, then said, "You and I both know he's no ordinary cat. He's resourceful and smart, and don't forget that he's also tough as nails."

I sniffed as the one person I loved most in this whole wide world soothed my tears. She would never even dream of lying to me. If she said Octo-Cat was going to be okay, then I knew he'd somehow find a way to get home again. We would find him, or he would find us. I simply couldn't accept any other outcome.

With great difficulty and a good deal of support from my nan, I finally headed to bed. Of course, Nan entered my tower bedroom several times throughout the night, making one ridiculous excuse after the other as to why she'd stopped in. It made me feel better, though, knowing she was there, that she'd always be there.

Even if Octo-Cat wasn't.

I hardly slept a wink, thinking every sound I heard might be Octo-Cat coming back to me. By the time the sun rose, I'd driven myself mad with worry.

A couple hours into the day, Nan came into my

room with a mug of coffee and a freshly baked scone and sat beside me petting my hair as she spoke. "I already called in sick to your work, and I figured since you're so sleepy, I can be the one to drive us around as we continue the search."

"Thank you, Nan," I managed around a deep yawn. I tried to stand but fell back toward the bed in exhaustion. My limbs simply felt too heavy to move all on my own.

"Sit for a spell," she instructed, tucking me back beneath the covers. "Finish your breakfast, and while you do that, I'll start calling around to all the local shelters."

She headed back toward the stairs, but I called for her to stop.

"Stay," I pleaded. "I don't think I can be alone."

"All righty, then." Nan nodded, settled herself at the end of my bed, and whipped out her cellphone. "We'll find him," she promised again as she placed a call to the first shelter on her list and waited through the rings.

One by one, the shelters all said they hadn't found our cat yet, but they would call if he turned up. With each failed outreach, my heart splintered even further. I needed to know that he was okay, that my rash decision hadn't cost him everything.

Once Nan had finished calling every shelter in the region, she placed her phone in my hands and said, "You should keep mine until you can get a new one. You need it more than I do."

I nodded and finished the coffee with a giant gulp, then tried to stand again. This time I didn't fall. Progress, at least.

"Let's get out there," I told Nan, reaching for the handrail to guide me safely down the stairs. "I can't wait another moment."

That was when the phone rang.

In my excitement to answer, I dropped it down the stairs.

Nan raced after it and managed to answer before the caller hung up. She faced me with wide, animated eyes as she spoke.

I stood at the top of the stairs and waited, trying not to get my hopes up too much.

A giant smile filled Nan's face as she said, "Yes, that sounds like our guy. We'll be there on the first ferry over."

She hung up and held the phone out to me as I raced down the stairs, stumbling as I went but not clumsily enough to fall. "Did somebody find him?"

Nan nodded brightly. "A small vet's office on Caraway Island of all places.

Caraway Island? How would he have gotten there? I know he wouldn't have braved that kind of swim, and the public ferry stopped running after eight o'clock.

"Someone definitely took him out there on purpose," I said through clenched teeth. "And I'm pretty sure I know exactly who did it."

"Oh, dear." Nan hummed a beat, then said, "Where are your priorities? First, let's bring our fella home, and then we can make sure those crooks pay."

We had to wait a solid hour for the next ferry, but the trip out to Blueberry Bay's only local island was a quick one at least. The vet's office wasn't hard to find, either.

"We scanned his microchip and called right away," one of the techs explained. Thank goodness I had updated the information to include both my number and Nan's after I'd officially adopted him. Otherwise they would have gotten a dead number that belonged to his dead former owner. I also wondered whether my phone was still active and if the bad guys still had it with them.

"Where is he?" I asked, glancing around the small office anxiously. "Is he okay? I can't wait to see him!"

Nan and I held hands while the tech returned to the back and then re-entered with a struggling Octo-Cat held in her arms. "He's got a bit of an attitude, this one," she said with a laugh.

"Octo-Cat!" I cried with relief. Yes, *cried.* I was crying yet again, but I was also far too happy to be embarrassed by it. "I missed you so much!"

He let me pick him up and even purred as I cuddled him to my chest.

"You had us really worried there, old boy," Nan said, giving him a scratch beneath his chin.

"Meow," he told her with a loving gaze. Nan always had been one of his favorites.

We thanked the vet and headed back to the parking lot. I couldn't wait to get the full story from Octo-Cat. As soon as we were all safely tucked within Nan's little red sports coupe, I placed him on my lap and said, "Tell us everything!"

He didn't answer; instead, he appeared tense as he stretched his head up carefully to peer out the front window.

"Octo-Cat," I said with a nervous laugh. "Stop being weird. We were so worried about you. I'm sorry about everything that happened, but I'm just so glad you're okay."

"Meow," he said sullenly.

"Hey, I know you're probably mad at me right now, but please, can you at least tell us what happened after the jewelry shop last night. You know, for Nan's sake?" I waited breathlessly. If he wanted to yell kitty curses at me, I would dutifully sit here and take it. After all, this was my fault. I deserved the worst.

Octo-Cat tilted his head to one side and meowed again.

That was when I realized the worst had already happened.

My cat could no longer understand me.

The magical residue that Moss had told me about had finally worn off. I'd lost the one thing that made me special, and with it, the best friend I had ever had. Something important in me had died, and I'd need a miracle to get it back.

Surely, there had to be a way.

I couldn't accept any other outcome.

We would fix this, Octo-Cat and me. We would fix everything.

Failure was simply not an option.

19

When we made it back home from our trip out to Caraway Island, a familiar Lexus sat waiting for us in the driveway. I'd seen it pretty much every day for the better part of the year and had no doubt that it belonged to Bethany, my frenemy turned boss.

I'd really thought we'd made great strides in our relationship. That is, until she hired Peter and refused to listen to any of my concerns.

She sat waiting in one of the rocking chairs Nan had added to the front porch earlier that summer. When we pulled up, she stood but didn't take any strides forward, instead waiting for us to join her on the porch.

"Take him inside," I told Nan, handing Octo-Cat

off to her. I was afraid to leave him alone since we'd picked him up. True, he'd lost his voice and not a limb, but the associated pain cut deeper than I could have ever imagined. I wondered if he knew, too.

"Come with your nan-nan, you sweet kitty boy," Nan cooed as she disappeared into the house. Although she understood that he and I had lost our special connection, Nan had never been able to talk to him, anyway. As far as their relationship was concerned, everything was perfectly normal. I knew he'd be happy with her. He'd always held a special place in his heart for Nan.

But without our ability to communicate, would he still hold one for me? I couldn't think like that. We'd find a way to fix everything. I had to believe in that, had to believe in us.

"What do you want?" I asked Bethany with a frown. I was both too exhausted and too devastated to play nice. I was also still more than a little miffed that she had been the one to bring Peter into my world.

"I'm assuming you heard about my cousin," she said, sitting back down and crossing her ankles like some kind of grand duchess.

I joined her by taking a seat in the other rocking

chair, mostly because I was too weary to keep standing on my own. “What about him? That he got arrested? Or that he’s responsible for the string of burglaries downtown? Oh, maybe you mean the fact that he can turn into a dog!”

Bethany sucked air in through her teeth. Her light blonde hair blew gently in the breeze, and she sat with one of her suit jackets draped across her lap, though it was far from chilly. Under any other circumstances, this would have been the perfect summer afternoon. As it was, though, this had become my own personal hell.

Just as Peter had promised if I pulled anything funny.

“Did you know?” I demanded of Bethany. “Did you know about all of this?”

She hung her head and nodded. “Yes, but I never thought he would hurt you, Angie. You have to believe me.”

“I thought we were friends,” I said coldly. Her betrayal stung. I couldn’t pretend that it hadn’t.

“We were,” she insisted, looking like she wanted to say something more, but stopping herself. She sighed and added, “Still are, I hope.”

I crossed my arms over my chest and refused to answer her either way. So much had already been taken from me that day. As much as I didn't want to lose anything else, I also didn't know if I'd ever be able to forgive Bethany for the things Peter had done. They never would have happened if she hadn't hired him in the first place or if she would have listened when I shared my concerns.

"Why are you here?" I demanded, not caring that my voice sounded cold and uncaring—or that she was technically my boss now.

"To help," she said softly. "And to explain a few things."

I made a dismissive motion with my hands. "Well, go ahead and get it over with, then."

"I hired Peter because I thought having an honest job would help him. I never meant for you to get hurt." She said so quickly it took me a moment to process. *"Please,* if you believe nothing else I say today, believe that."

I considered this but kept quiet, waiting for her to offer more. I wasn't sure any explanation would ever be enough, but at least someone was finally giving me answers without threatening or hurting me in the process.

"I knew he'd been hanging out with some less than savory characters, but I had no idea just how deeply he was involved. I had hoped it wasn't too late to save him, but apparently I was wrong." Most of the women I knew would cry to gain sympathy, but not Bethany. She remained stoic to the bitter end. Always had.

"Did you know about the magic?" I demanded.

"*Yes,*" she said emphatically. She clenched her eyes shut then admitted, "Because I have it, too."

I stared at her with my mouth hanging open rather impolitely. Of course she did. They were cousins, after all. "Do you use it to rob people, too?" I asked with a snort.

"No," she insisted, shaking her head. "I don't use it at all."

"What about the essential oils?" I mumbled, thinking back to all of the strangeness Bethany had exhibited since I've known her. As far as I knew, she was perfectly normal other than her obsession with mixing and matching scents each morning. "Are those your potions or brews or whatever?"

I laughed bitterly at this, but Bethany remained firm.

"I'm not a witch," she told me. "Mostly because witches aren't real."

"How can I believe you, though? Up until a few days ago, I didn't even know that magic was real." I paused a moment to let that sink in. "Where does it end? How do I even know what's real and what's made up now?"

"You can't," she said sadly. "And I'm sorry that you've been pulled into this world. I never wanted that for you."

"Then what were you doing this whole time?" I couldn't take her at face value. Not anymore. I'd seen too much to ever trust anyone at their word again. "Were you lying in wait until the timing was right?"

She looked truly pained, but only a small part of me cared. I'd been hurt, too. Burned. Damaged beyond repair.

"Just trying to live a normal life, the same as you."

"But you're one of them," I reminded her.

"Not all magic people are bad."

"Peter's bad."

"Yes," she confirmed with a sigh. "I wanted more for him, but I was too late to help."

We sat in silence for a few moments as the wind blew the overgrown blades of grass in a wave across my front lawn.

"Have you ever wondered why you can talk to your cat?" Bethany asked, her eyes full of unshed tears. She was still too tough to cry. That was another thing about us that was irreconcilably different.

I cried freely. Why even fight it anymore? "You know about that?" I asked, too exhausted to be shocked by anything now.

She nodded, then raised the suit jacket from her lap and tossed it to me. "Do you recognize this?"

"It's one of your ugly blazers."

"I'll let that slide, because I know you're hurting right now," she said, waiting.

I fingered the cool fabric, releasing the scents of juniper and lemon into the air.

"Do you remember wearing it?" she pressed again.

I thought back to one of the many times Thompson had forced me to borrow clothes from Bethany to appear more presentable when an important client visited the office.

And that was when the final piece of this week's horrible puzzle settled into place. "Ethel Fulton's will reading," I said.

"Yes," she said with a nod of affirmation. "Do you understand what happened now?"

"The magical residue Moss mentioned. That was from you?"

She nodded again. "It was in my blazer. The

electric shock strengthened it, transferred that energy to you."

"But I'm not magical," I said with a huff.

"No, not fully. Usually resonance disappears quickly. The fact yours didn't is my fault, I'm afraid."

I turned to her with a hundred questions begging to be let out. A single word escaped my lips. *"Why?"*

"I already told you, I don't practice magic. The energy has nowhere to go. A lot of it has built up over the years, packed in tight. That zap uncoiled all of it and created a reaction."

"But I can't mess with people's minds or use glamor or change into an animal." I felt so incredibly small and helpless as I reminded her of all the things I couldn't do. Ever since I'd gained the ability to speak to Octo-Cat, I'd thought of myself as having superpowers. What a joke. There were real super humans out there in the world, but sadly, I wasn't one of them.

"You got a small but powerful dose from that jacket," Bethany explained, watching me carefully. "The cat got it, too."

I searched her face while she struggled to find her words.

"He was close by and somehow it created a bond between you. I don't know why you only got the one ability or why it hasn't left you yet."

"Oh, but Bethany," I said, once again crying for all I'd lost. "It has. Octo-Cat and I... We can't talk anymore."

Then I realized something wonderful. "Can you fix it? Can you make things how they were again?"

Bethany bit her lower lip and sucked a deep breath in through her nostrils. "I don't use magic," she said again. "But for you, I'm willing to try."

20

"The cruel irony is that the less one practices magic, the stronger she becomes," Bethany explained as we settled into my home library side-by-side. Octo-Cat sat on my lap, but I'd asked Nan to sit this one out. As much as I loved her, I felt this moment needed to be private.

"It's all part of the great balance," Bethany continued as I stared at the trees swaying in the gentle winds outside. "It helps to keep the power-hungry from becoming too powerful. Keeps the magic world hidden and safe."

"Moss mentioned some of this," I said, nodding along as I recalled my time in the fishbowl.

"As I already said outside, the fact that I'm a

non-practitioner makes my magic abnormally strong," Bethany continued. "But I'm not an expert in harnessing it. I can try to transfer some of it back to you, but it might not work." She swallowed hard. "You could also get hurt."

"It's worth the risk," I said without hesitation, petting Octo-Cat as I spoke. "I'm ready."

"Our best chance at getting this to work right is to recreate the scene at the will reading as closely as possible. That's why I brought you the jacket." She nodded toward the blazer which sat crumpled in my lap, then picked up the reusable cloth shopping bag she'd brought inside with her.

The moment I saw what came out of that bag, I jumped to my feet in sheer terror. "Keep that thing away from me!" I screamed as I stared at the old office coffee maker, refusing to so much as blink until it was safely put away. It had almost killed me the first time, and I didn't doubt it could finish the job today.

"We need to recreate what happened that day," Bethany reminded me. "I'm sorry, but it's the most surefire way to get this to work."

I shivered violently as I regarded the evil appliance. Could I do this? Could I face this deep-seated, albeit very rational, fear and live to tell the tale?

Octo-Cat meowed and rubbed himself against my ankles. When I reached down to pet him, I found that he was purring. He gave me a sandpaper kiss, then jumped back into the window seat and rubbed his head against the coffee maker, keeping his eyes on me the whole time.

I smiled despite my fear. "If he believes this will work, then so do I. Um, do you mind if I close my eyes first?"

"Do whatever you need to do," Bethany said, situating the coffee maker near the closest outlet. "I took the liberty of fraying the power cord some. Thought it might make for an easier electrocution."

Oh, joy.

Octo-Cat mewled again. He believed in me, believed in us. I'd do anything to protect that even if it meant walking head-first into danger—which, apparently, it did.

Bethany put both hands on my shoulders, and I felt a warm, pleasant sensation transfer from her to me through the blazer. "Are you ready?" she asked, pulling her hands away.

I nodded, clenching my eyes tight as she guided me toward the coffee-making death trap. Octo-Cat stayed at my side every step of the way, and when I couldn't find the cord with my eyes still closed, he pushed my hand in the right direction.

There was only one thing left to do.

With a deep breath—one I hoped wouldn't be my last—I picked up the power cord and jammed it into the outlet. When the burst of electricity shot through my body, I collapsed and fell unconscious with a smile.

* * *

"Angie? Angie? Are you okay?" Bethany asked, cradling my head in her lap as I came to.

"What happened?" I asked. My mind felt... fuzzy.

"Did it work?" she asked excitedly, disregarding my question entirely.

Bethany helped me sit up, and I glanced around the room. We were at my house in the library I had claimed as my own special sanctuary. But why?

Octo-Cat approached me carefully, almost as if he could catch whatever I had. "Yuck," he said. "You still smell like that basement."

Tears filled my eyes and suddenly I remembered everything. "You can talk," I said, sobbing freely.

Bethany cheered and pumped a fist in the air.

Octo-Cat shook his head in amazement. "Of course I can talk. I've always been able to talk. But now you can listen again. Oh my whiskers, I have so much to tell you."

"It worked," I sobbed. "I'm magic again."

Bethany placed a gentle hand on my shoulder. "I think you've got it all wrong. Don't you see? You're not magic, but the bond you two share is."

"This sounds like an episode of the *Care Bears,*" I quipped.

"My Little Pony would be the more recent reference," Bethany said with a shrug. "But sure, *Care Bears,* yeah."

I gave her a tight hug despite the fact sarcasm simply dripped off her. "Thank you so much for helping us."

"Hey, don't get too friendly there," Octo-Cat warned as he wrinkled his nose in disgust. "She's a dog, too."

"You're a dog? Like Peter?" I asked.

She nodded. "I can become a pit bull. I did it a few times in my school days to scare bullies away. *Bully breed,* indeed," she said with a dry chuckle.

"So what happens now?" I wanted to know.

Bethany sighed and looked toward the door. “Unfortunately, I need to go.”

“Okay, but I’ll see you at work tomorrow, right?”

She shook her head. “I have to leave Glendale, I mean. Now that magic has been exposed, it isn’t safe.”

I’d be sad to see Bethany leave but understood her position. “What about Peter and Moss? Are they going, too?”

“Peter’s coming with me just as soon as I bail him out. Moss, on the other hand, will... Well, he’ll be around for a while.”

“Why? What happened?”

“Peter turned Moss in to the cops so that he could plea out of felony charges.”

“Figures,” I scoffed, thinking of neither man-animal fondly now that the worst was over.

“I’m taking him to Georgia. It’s kind of like the magic capital of the world.”

“Atlanta?”

“No, a much smaller town called Peach Plains.”

“Can you do me a favor before you go?”

“I’ll help however I can, but remember, my magic isn’t very focused.”

“Can you do that memory thing on me?” I

begged her to understand. This was the only option for me now.

Bethany stared at me in confusion. "Why would you want that?"

I shrugged even though I'd already made up my mind and knew I wouldn't be changing it any time soon. "I liked the world better when it made more sense. If the magic is leaving, anyway, then I think I'd rather not remember it."

Bethany thought about this for a second before nodding her agreement. "But you do understand that you also won't remember why you can talk to your cat? And that if anything ever goes wrong again, you won't know who to turn to for help?"

I considered this, but it wasn't enough of an argument to sway me. "We've become good friends. Haven't we, Bethany?"

Bethany smiled at me and gave me a quick hug. "Of course."

"Then just check in on us every so often. Make sure we're okay."

"I can definitely do that," she promised. "Now, before I try this, you're sure you want to forget all of it?"

"All the magic stuff, if you'd please."

Bethany raised one hand and made the whirling

hand gesture I'd seen both Peter and Moss use before. Soon I wouldn't remember any of it.

I watched her fingers dance gracefully before me. Bethany had always been so delicate and dainty. It was pretty hilarious that she could secretly turn into a pit bull. I liked knowing that, even if it wouldn't last much longer...

"There," Bethany said, blinking at me curiously. "How do you feel now?"

"A bit light-headed," I answered, wondering why I suddenly felt so dizzy. "Can we open up the window and get some air flowing through here?"

"Sure," she said, kneeling down on my cushy window seat and cranking the glass open. Funny, I couldn't even remember asking her over, let alone what we'd discussed during our visit so far.

"Ahh, what a beautiful day it's turned out to be," Octo-Cat said, inhaling the sweet summer air.

We both stuck our noses out and took deep, contented breaths. I closed my eyes and let the sun kiss my face. What a perfect day it had been. I couldn't remember much about it, but knew I was happy—and also that I was blessed beyond measure.

"What's that cat doing?" someone asked from so close it startled me.

"Do you think he's going to eat us?" another voice wondered aloud.

"Stop asking questions and fly away to safety," a third said.

I opened my eyes just in time to see a trio of gulls launch themselves off the roof.

I desperately wanted to ask Octo-Cat if he'd heard them, too, but Bethany still stood nearby and she didn't know our secret.

I knew one thing for sure, though. Those birds had talked...

And I'd understood every word they'd said.

What's even worse than having a snarky talking tabby as your best friend? When he inexplicably goes missing...

CLICK HERE to get your copy of *The Cat Caper,* so that you can keep reading this series today!

* * *

Pssst... If you absolutely loved this book and want even more, check out Molly's Cozy Kitty Club for behind-the-scenes trivia and bonus scenes you won't find anywhere else!

WHAT'S NEXT?

What's even worse than having a snarky talking tabby as your best friend?

When he inexplicably goes missing...

Octo-Cat is gone, and all the evidence suggests that he was taken on purpose. With the growing number of people the two of us have put behind bars, it's no surprise that someone's out for revenge.

But how will I ever manage to solve this particular crime without the help of my partner?

The only other person who might be able to help me just relocated to Georgia. But I'm desperate enough to try anything, including exposing my secret to the whole of Blueberry Bay. Anything to bring him home safe.

Oh, Octo-Cat. Where have you gone?

THE CAT CAPER is now available.

CLICK HERE to get your copy so that you can keep reading this series today!

SNEAK PEEK

THE CAT CAPER

My name's Angie Russo, and I'm a cat person.

Lately, that is the most important thing about me.

Not that I'm a part-time paralegal and also a part-time private investigator. Not that I live in a giant East Coast manor house or that my quirky nan is one of my best friends. Not even the fact that I've managed to rack up seven associate degrees due to my academic indecisiveness.

Nope.

The most important thing about me is definitely the fact that I have a cat.

But he's not just any ordinary feline, mind you.

He talks. *A lot.* As in hardly ever shuts up.

And if you think your cat is demanding, just imagine what my life looks like.

I have to feed him a particular brand of food in a particular flavor in a particular Lenox dish and at very particular times of days. He also only drinks Evian. I've tried to trick him in the past to save on this ridiculous expense, but—I kid you not—he knew the difference. And, boy, did I pay for that one.

In all honesty, I can spare the expense, though. You see, my cat also has a trust fund—a big one. His previous owner was murdered, and it was by pure dumb luck that he and I ended up together. That is, if you can call almost dying at the hands of a faulty coffee maker "luck."

I mean, I do.

I love my life and would change very little about it. I do plan to quit my paralegal gig soon to pursue detective work full-time. Naturally, my cat would be my partner in that operation. He watches so much *Law & Order* that he practically has an honorary degree in criminal justice, and he's got claws that he isn't afraid to use when we find ourselves in a tricky scrape.

Other than his sometimes gratuitous violence and over-the-top television addiction, he has plenty of other unique skills that make him an indispensable partner, too. First, there's the fact we can communicate. Obviously, no one ever suspects that the curious-looking feline across the way is actually listening in on their conversations.

When you add Nan to the mix with her background in Broadway and knack for creating colorful characters and then bringing them to life flawlessly, we have quite the little operation.

So, go ahead and eat your heart out, Scooby Doo.

If you're wondering about me and who I am outside of being a cat owner, I'll make this real simple for you: I'm the Velma of the group. I love researching, learning, wrapping my mind around any and every puzzle that comes our way.

I have a near photographic memory and a knack for mnemonic devices, but lately my brain has been a tad less reliable than I'd like.

Usually, I remember everything without fail. Ever since this new guy Peter Peters started working at the law office, though, things have definitely gotten a bit fuzzy. I hated that guy almost instantly, and I'm pretty sure he has something to do with the fog that's taken up residence in my head... But I just can't remember why.

Lucky for me, he'll be leaving the state very soon. Unluckily, he's taking his cousin Bethany, a former partner at the same firm, with him. She was a good friend, and I'll definitely miss having her around. Still, I get the fact that she needs to be there for her family—even if this particular member of her family is the creepiest guy I have ever met in my entire life.

Honestly, it's probably time for me to quit, anyway. Well, just as soon as I work up the nerve to let down my secret crush by handing in my two weeks' notice. I've had the hots for our senior partner, Charles Longfellow, III, ever since he moved here from California and began working his way up the ranks at our firm. He's only a few years older than me, a legal prodigy and also someone who's had a few lucky strokes like I have—so no judgement, please.

I'd probably have bitten the bullet and asked him out by now, but he has a girlfriend now. By the way, I hate her and not just because she's standing in the way of what I'm convinced could actually be true love, but because she's mean and bitter and has never shown me an ounce of kindness in our entire acquaintanceship.

At least she's not a murderer, although I did

suspect her of a double homicide a few months back. We solved that one, though, and got both her and her brother off the hook. We also solved the murder of a prominent senator who used to live right next door.

And as ready as I am to hang up my sign as a full time P.I., I'd much rather be chasing white-collar criminals around town than the homicidal maniacs I've been dealing with as of late. Because that's the thing about murderers, they're dangerous with a capital *D.* It stands to reason that eventually one of them is going to want revenge on the crazy girl and her cat that got them arrested in the first place.

I just hope I'm ready when karma comes calling...

I almost ran straight into Nan when I returned home from work that sunny afternoon.

"Look what I made for you today in my community art class!" she cried, completely unbothered by the fact I'd almost knocked her into the antique stained-glass windows that flanked either side of our front door.

I took one giant step back and studied the sizable metal sign she held between her aged hands.

"Pet Whisperer, P.I." I read aloud, then grabbed the thing to take a closer look—and almost dropped it as soon as the heft transferred to my hands. "Oof, this is really heavy!"

Nan shook her head and tutted at me. "Well, it's not made of paper, dear."

"What kind of art class are you taking, anyway?" I said as I appreciated how the various scrap metals had come together to create something new and beautiful.

"It's a little bit of everything—sculpture, welding, landscapes, still-lifes, nudes." She winked at that last one, and I had no idea that meant it was her entire reason for signing up in the first place.

"Sounds like a good time," I said with a laugh. My nan was always finding something new and exciting to occupy her time. Apparently, this included advertising my closely kept secret to all of Blueberry Bay.

Nan caught me studying the sign with a nervous expression and explained, "It's for your business, dear. Seeing as I'm your assistant, I figured I'd make myself useful."

"But we haven't even officially opened yet," I argued. I loved Nan and was excited she wanted to help, but the added pressure didn't make this big career transition any easier on me.

"Yes, you really do need to get on with it, already," my grandmother told me as she furrowed her brow in my direction.

I groaned even though she was one-hundred percent right about this. "Okay, but I don't want people to know I talk to animals, remember?" That was the other weird thing about the last couple weeks.

My memory was a bit fuzzy, but also my mind seemed to be more open. I still didn't know how I could talk to Octo-Cat, but lately I'd been able to hear other animals besides him, too.

First there were the birds on the rooftop, then a curious squirrel in my garden. I'd even managed to listen in on a great, big buck I'd startled in the woods outside our manor house. My ability to understand other animals was touch and go, and also a brand new complication in my already crazy life.

It had always been Octo-Cat and only Octo-Cat, and I really didn't know how I felt about becoming a full-on Dr. Doolittle these days. If word spread among the animal kingdom that I could understand their needs, would they all start swarming me with their legal problems?

I was way out of my depth here, considering I was just a paralegal and had no great passion for the law—other than choosing to uphold it most of the time in my day-to-day life.

"Where's Octo-Cat?" I asked, craning my neck to glance up the grand staircase but not finding him at the top. Normally, he liked hanging out up there this time of day because it was when the skylights dumped lots of warm sunlight in that exact spot.

"He's around here somewhere, I'm sure," Nan answered dismissively as she took the sign back from me and studied it with a huge, self-satisfied grin on her face.

"When did you last see him?" I asked, checking his other favorite nap spots. Maybe the sun wasn't following its normal, predictable pattern today. Perhaps cloud cover had interfered. I knew my cat well enough to know he hadn't voluntarily changed his routine.

Something was off, and the sooner I figured out what that was, the better I'd feel going into the rest of the day.

Nan came over and gave my shoulder a little

squeeze. "I watched an episode of *Criminal Intent* with him during my mid-morning tea. That was only a little more than two hours ago. I'm sure he's fine, dear."

But I wasn't. Not at all.

I'd already lost him briefly a couple weeks ago, when he'd ended up on Caraway Island as if by magic. I still had no idea how he'd gotten out there or why I couldn't remember going with Nan to pick him up. All I knew is I needed to find my cat, and I needed to find him now.

"Help me look for him. Would you?" I asked Nan.

She nodded and tucked the metal sign away in the closet, then together we conducted a thorough search of both the house and the yard.

"Well, that's strange," Nan said, scratching her forehead. "Maybe he's just out for a walk and lost track of time."

Again, this was not how my cat operated. If I so much as tried to sleep in an extra minute, I'd get an earful about how disappointed he was in me. He did use his cat door as Nan suggested, but he never strayed far.

At least not until today.

A swash of white appeared at the bottom of the

driveway, and I watched as the mail truck grew closer and closer.

"Beautiful day, isn't it?" the mail lady, Julie, trilled as she rummaged through her sack. "A light load today," she said next as she handed me a stack of mail that had been folded together using a thin rubber band.

"Thank you, Julie!" I called after her, biting my lip as I quickly flipped through the junk mail, bills, and solicitations.

But then I found an unfamiliar envelope, one that had no return address and was addressed simply to *Octavius Fulton.*

Yes, to my cat.

I swallowed hard and tore it open without even the slightest moment's hesitation...

What happens next?
Don't wait to find out...

Purchase your copy so that you can keep reading this zany mystery series today!

MORE MOLLY

ABOUT MOLLY FITZ

While USA Today bestselling author Molly Fitz can't technically talk to animals, she and her three feline writing assistants have deep and very animated conversations as they navigate their days.

She lives with her comedian husband, diva daughter, and their own private zoo somewhere in the wilds of Alaska. Molly will occasionally venture out for good food, great coffee, or to meet new animal friends.

Learn more about Molly and her books, and be sure to sign up for her newsletter at **www.MollyMysteries.com**!

PET WHISPERER P.I.

Angie Russo just partnered up with Blueberry Bay's first ever talking cat detective. Along with his ragtag gang of human and animal helpers, Octo-Cat is determined to save the day… so long as it doesn't interfere with his schedule. Start with book 1, ***Kitty Confidential***.

MERLIN THE MAGICAL FLUFF

Gracie Springs is not a witch… but her cat is. Now she must help to keep his secret or risk spending the rest of her life in some magical prison. Too bad trouble seems to find them at every turn! Start with book 1, ***Merlin the Magical Fluff***.

PARANORMAL TEMP AGENCY

Tawny Bigford's simple life takes a turn for the magical when she stumbles upon her landlady's murder and is recruited by a talking black cat named Fluffikins to take over the deceased's role as the official Town Witch for Beech Grove, Georgia. Start with book 1, ***Witch for Hire***.

CLAW & ORDER

Moss O'Malley isn't a real cat, and he's not a real cop either. Yet here here he is, serving and protecting while stuck in this suit of fur. That's what happens when you're a shifter con man who's been caught in the act. He's no narc, but he'll also do whatever it takes to stay out of that horrible cat rescue-slash-prison. Start with book 1, ***Paws & Probable Cause***.

THE MYSTERIES OF MOONLIGHT MANOR (WITH TRIXIE SILVERTALE)

Sydney Coleman has it all—until she doesn't. No sooner does she launch her bed and breakfast, than a trio of ghosts turn up oppose her at every turn. They insist she solve the murder of their mistress, but Sydney is desperate for cash. If she can't book some guests fast, her haunted mansion is utterly doomed. Start with book 1, ***Moonlight & Mischief***.

THE MEOWING MEDIUM (WITH L.A. BORUFF)

Mags McAllister lives a simple life making candles for tourists in historic Larkhaven, Georgia. But when a cat with mismatched eyes enters her life, she finds herself with the ability to see into the realm of spirits... Now the ghosts of people long dead have started coming to her for help solving their cold cases. Start with book 1, ***Secrets of the Specter***.

CONNECT WITH MOLLY

Sign up for my newsletter and get a special digital prize pack for joining, including an exclusive story, Meowy Christmas Mayhem, fun quiz, and lots of cat pictures!

mollymysteries.com/subscribe

Have you ever wanted to talk to animals? You can chat with Octo-Cat and help him solve an exclusive online mystery here:

mollymysteries.com/chat

JOIN MOLLY'S READER CLUB

If you ever wished you could converse with cats, here's your opportunity! This is me officially inviting you into my whacky inner world as part of my Cozy Kitty Club.

For those who just can't get enough of my zany cat characters and their hapless humans, this club will provide weekly (sometimes daily) new content to devour.

From early access to exclusive stories, behind-the-scenes trivia to never-before-released bonus content, and even some signed books and swag thrown in for fun, the CKC has a lot to love.

Come check it out at **www.MollyMysteries.com/club**.

MORE BOOKS LIKE THIS

Welcome to Whiskered Mysteries, where each and every one of our charming cozies comes with a furry sidekick... or several! Around here, you'll find we're all about crafting the ultimate reading experience. Whether that means laugh-out-loud antics, jaw-dropping magical exploits, or whimsical journeys through small seaside towns, you decide.

So go on and settle into your favorite comfy chair and grab one of our *paw*some cozy mysteries to kick off your next great reading adventure!

Visit our website to browse our books and meet our authors, to jump into our discussion group, or to join our newsletter. See you there!

www.WhiskeredMysteries.com

Made in the USA
Las Vegas, NV
09 August 2023